OUT OF THE
Shadows

A NOVEL BY
SUSAN EVANS McCLOUD

BOOKCRAFT
SALT LAKE CITY, UTAH

All characters in this book are fictitious,
and any resemblance to actual persons,
living or dead, is purely coincidental.

Library of Congress Catalog Card Number 98-74083
ISBN 1-57008-571-4

First Printing, 1998

Printed in the United States of America

For

My daughter,
Morag Elizabeth Jessie

with whom—in all things of heart
and spirit—I am one

❧ Chapter One ❧

THERE ARE FATES WORSE THAN DEATH, though Isabel wouldn't have said so. Both her parents died when she was a child, and she considered death a disgrace, a failure of sorts. Aunt Gwen had pronounced it thus upon many an occasion, tsk-tsking her tongue, scolding Isa's father for succumbing and her mother for resigning. Life, first and foremost, is duty—and death, especially an early death, plays havoc with that.

Isabel had never expected much out of life beyond duty: Aunt Gwen had made sure of this, too. "Mortality is a veil of tears," she often said, pursing her mouth into a tight, unpleasant expression. "We are here to endure and prove ourselves worthy"—though Isa had never figured out quite what she meant by that. "We must take what God hands out to us, child, and be grateful."

Grateful? Aunt Gwen did not seem grateful; she always seemed sour and disapproving. *Grateful?* Isabel wondered every time she heard the word. Grateful for what? This narrow existence with a straight-laced, bitter old woman—this absence of laughter and promise?

"Beauty is more often a curse than a blessing," her aunt had lectured her. "Why, look at your dear mother."

Look at her mother! Isabel wished she could. All she possessed was one small, faded photograph taken when Jean Emerson was a girl of sixteen. The face that stared out at her from under the wide brim of a summer bonnet was sweet, but Isa couldn't say if it was beautiful.

"God did not see fit to bestow much beauty upon you, child, so you must make yourself useful. You cannot expect young men to flock round you as they did your mother and a husband to come at you whistling. You shall have to find a means of supporting yourself."

Dismal prospect, or at least it was meant to be so. Yet Isabel always did well in school. She liked to learn, preferring reading to the tedium of handwork; indeed, to stitching and sewing of any kind. The first public school in the entire Western Hemisphere was opened in Boston in 1635 and now, in 1899, more educational opportunities were afforded women here than in most places. Still, Aunt Gwendolyn was surprised when she won a place for herself at Boston College; but Isa was not. She distinguished herself in literature and earned a teacher's certificate before she was twenty-one, and life on the whole looked promising. But that was over six years ago.

Isabel sighed and poked at the mound of thick summer grass with the toe of her shoe. The Common was unusually lovely today; cool and shaded, removed from the noise and bustle of Charles Street and Boylston Street that sided it. Here her cares, heavy though they were, floated upward to dissipate among the dense leafy branches of the elm and planer trees that so mercifully shut out the sun. Here she could forget her humiliation and the pressing need to do something about it. Here respite, like the temperate air that cooled her skin, smoothed out the knots that constricted her chest, and made it possible to breathe again. She closed her eyes and wished she could sit there forever, never stirring; never thinking or feeling at all.

"You most certainly will go to meeting, young lady." Aunt Gwendolyn's tone was curt; the sound of it curdled, like a piece of tainted meat, in Isabel's stomach.

"I am no longer a child," she responded, chafing at the inflexible restraint so severely applied. "I am a woman full grown."

"You are still under my roof, missy," Aunt Gwen snapped back, not in the least nonplussed. "And, as long as you are, you will defer to my wishes and counsel."

Isa shut her lips tight against the injustice, knowing the hasty retort she was wishing to speak would do her more harm than good. She was trembling inside, as though she were seventeen again, and on the verge of weak tears. *I simply do not know if I can bear it!* she longed to cry out. *Have compassion upon me!* But the expression on her aunt's face stopped her; it was so closed, so forbidding, that she turned away with a sigh.

"Don't be so touchy, Isabel," Gwendolyn shot after her. "No one really cares the way you suppose they do. And if those who should be your friends mock and judge you, the sin be upon their own heads."

Isabel nodded woodenly. She felt dull inside, as though someone had wrapped wool around her vitals, around her heart, smothering all sensation. If only she could keep that feeling, to carry her through the service, through the stares and snickers, the glances of pity—through seeing Lawrence there with another.

But it happened much as she had fore-dreaded. Aunt Gwendolyn was punctual, so they were seated in their own pew in time to watch the grand arrival of the Nicholson girls—a mother and four sisters—with Lawrence the only male, leading the train with his mother on his right arm and a Nicholson-to-be on his left. Miss Blanche Bradstreet walked with her nose a bit high and her eyes straight ahead.

She is lovely, Isa thought, *and much closer to his age. Fair hair and fair eyes, and fair prospects.* Twenty-seven was over a quarter of a century; she should have listened to her aunt and not expected to be looked upon as an object of romance by a man nearly half a dozen years younger than herself. Yet, it was his mother who had done this. She would have none of it. Her only son must marry to advantage, and Isabel did not meet any of the requirements; thus she must be disposed of with dispatch.

It was just as she had imagined: people crowding around the new couple as soon as the service was finished, cheerful questions and congratulations, and squeals of delight. Nor did she escape the sharp-honed ruthlessness of those narrow women who could not resist an opportunity to probe the tender wound by addressing cruel, pointed questions to her—their faces bland and innocuous, while their words pierced deep: "Isabel, dear, so sorry to hear of the breaking off of your engagement . . . and such a promising young gentleman, too"—with a glance in Lawrence's direction. Or: "So, your beau has found a new flame. Well, gentlemen are like that, aren't they—always the new young thing drawing their eye away."

Isa had always wondered what caused people to be unkind to one another for no cause at all. Her own response to the misfortunes of others was usually a swift pricking of commiserate pain, and a vague sense of discomfort at being reminded of the sorrows this old world harbored. She knew the sort of people who gloated over her disappointment were not worth taking notice of, not worth being hurt by—she knew so in her head. But her heart was too tender to reject even the slightest wound inflicted upon it right now.

Lawrence did not glance once in her direction; he most assuredly had stern instructions from his mother. Those dark penciled eyebrows remained poised above lowered lashes; his finely molded profile was all he showed her. Isabel slipped out ahead of Aunt Gwendolyn, as soon as she could extricate herself from the curious, and took a cab from the Old South Meeting House, where anti-British rhetoric had once fired the populace, down Washington to Essex and to the modest brownstone where she had lived for as long as she could remember. Boston. The Cradle of Liberty—the Athens of America. Isabel had grown up reading about Boston in the history books, not only in primary school, but in her university classes as well. She was proud to be a Bostonian. She loved every square inch of the history that was thick in the air here and set this city apart. She had never wanted to live anywhere else and now, suddenly, all she could think of was getting away.

It wouldn't have happened, Isabel mused, *if Lawrence's mother had not taken a grand tour across Europe that had lasted nearly nine months. He was free to be himself then, and he fell in love with me, fair and square, before she returned to fill his head with social obligation and familial duty and the horror of tainting his bloodline and jeopardizing his inheritance.*

She shivered, though the night was warm and she had a wrap round her shoulders. She had worn her best silk frock, cream colored, with a ruche at her throat trimmed with thin lilac ribbons and sleeves bordered with the same ruche of crepe de chine and ribbon. She generally avoided the extreme in her attire, but she knew the milky cream of this particular dress set off her dark hair and eyes, making a stunning contrast. She had a right to look stunning for once, especially now, when all eyes would be turned with critical appraisal upon her.

Oh, how little any of that had mattered when she and Lawrence were alone! He had a fine mind and a gentle sense of humor. They had discussed literature and politics, spent afternoons at the museum, evenings at lectures or concerts. He was refined, of course, and impeccably educated, but she had been able to get past that, and she liked what she had discovered beneath the veneer. *Now it all will belong to another,* she thought, and the thick moist air of the summer evening seemed to clot in her throat.

I must get away. The thought itself was an infidelity that Isa shrank from. Had not her own people met at Fanueil Hall and fought at Bunker Hill, worshiped in the Old South Meeting House, started a blacksmith shop and a mercantile, and been laid to rest beside Sam Adams and Paul Revere in the Old Granary Burying Ground? She was part of a fabric, tightly woven and proudly worn. *I can carry it with me,* she thought. *Wrap it around as protection.*

That night, after blowing out the candle, Isabel knelt by her bedside. The loneliness that gnawed at her insides was painful. *Help me find someplace to go,* she prayed, *the right place, if it matters. Help me to find some purpose, some real use to my life.*

She knelt for a long time. When she opened her eyes, the moon had cast a pattern across her coverlet; a gentle criss-crossing of limbs of the apple tree outside her window, heavy and swaying in the night breeze, in bars of gold against the white cloth. She traced the outline with the tip of one finger. *Have I the courage to go, God,* she breathed, *even if you show me the way?*

❧ Chapter Two ❧

THE OLD CORNER BOOKSTORE, AT THE meeting of Washington and Beacon Streets, was crowded with the usual array of businessmen, professors, and students, with a budding writer or two drawing a small group in a hopeful huddle, conversation rising and falling in a pleasant undertone. Isabel worked her way through to the shelf where the daily newspapers were displayed and stretched to pull down a copy of the *Boston Globe*. She paid the clerk, then found an empty wing-backed easy chair and dropped down gratefully, settling her skirts around her and beginning at once to thumb through the thin pages until she came to the classified section. There were many advertisements from a variety of sources; she began a methodical review. Most of the posts being offered were in eastern seaboard cities. A few ranged into the midwest—Chicago, Cincinnati, one from a school in Denver. But Isabel did not wish to go west. Mathematics and science; English teachers must be in good supply just now. She sighed audibly. The list was suddenly beginning to thin, narrow down to less possibilities than she had expected. She tucked a stray lock of hair beneath the brim of her bonnet and turned the page. Then she saw it: a small advertisement boxed round in black lines, so that it stood out a bit from the others. Isa put her hand to her throat, where she could feel the beating of her pulse, like the anxious fluttering of wings.

> *British Girls' School in Yorkshire desires the services of an American teacher: preferably female, preferably educated in English and the humanities, to begin Michaelmas term, first of October. Send credentials and references to:*

A name and address followed, but Isabel scarcely saw them. She knew at once that she had stumbled upon the thing she desired— the answer she sought. *England! The old world!* Why had she not thought of it?

Yorkshire. Her mind was racing still. That meant the moors Charlotte Brontë had described so vividly. She would rather find a post by the sea, but . . . Isabel laughed to herself. Nothing on the island of Britain was very far from the ocean; it didn't matter at all. Just to be there, to feast on the age-old history and culture. How often did the British *request* an American? They usually showed only disdain for "the colonists," as they called her countrymen still. *I will go. It must be me*, Isabel determined. She folded the paper and tucked it into her satchel. Then she rose and left with such a determined air that several pairs of eyes followed her progress along the narrow store aisles, wondering with idle curiosity upon what manner of errand the young lady was bent.

Isabel made a quick round, requesting her records from the school board who had hired her, her transcripts and credentials from Boston College, references from former teachers and colleagues, as well as from a few select students who had already begun to distinguish themselves in the arena of Boston business and politics. It was not an unpleasant process; everyone seemed pleased to accommodate her.

She arrived home in a state of excitement, not the least bit tired, but hard-pressed to conceal her mood from Aunt Gwenie. The summer afternoon seemed all aglow. As soon as their modest meal had been eaten, consisting of greens from the garden and fresh cod baked in a cream sauce, Isa helped wash up the dishes, then excused herself as calmly as she could. "I am spending the evening at the library," she said, which was the truth.

"Preparing for classes so soon? It's only mid-June, Isabel. Really, you'll ruin your eyesight."

Isabel sighed. She had been prepared to feel sorry for her little deceits, for her secret plans. But Aunt Gwen's criticism always had a withering effect upon her and, in this case, merely firmed her resolve and made her feel justified in following her own lights. *Each human being must do so, sooner or later*, Isabel kept reminding herself. *I wish it were not so hard for me to stand on my own feet and do what my own desires dictate.*

Even her first teaching position had been secured through Aunt Gwen; she had a friend who would be happy to use his influence. Isabel could have found a job on her own, and wanted to, but it had been easier to go along with Aunt Gwendolyn than to oppose.

She wondered, as she had countless times, about her mother. She felt certain Aunt Gwen had dominated her, too.

"Your father left his wife, when he had no business doing so." That was all Aunt Gwendolyn would ever tell her. "Where else did Jean have to go—who else to turn to?"

She must have hated it, Isabel would think, watching her stern, starched aunt go about her household chores, her movements brusque and efficient. *She had been a wife, with her own household, her own ways, then had to submit to this domination, this eagle eye watching her, always watching her. She was young, this Jean with the sweet, laughing eyes. Did she feel stifled and smothered as I?*

In the dim, musty interior of the library, Isabel composed a letter to accompany her credentials, attempting to convey to the Mr. Peter Hay of the advertisement the extent of her interest without sounding too eager. Perhaps her age and experience would serve her well, for once. Certainly they would not wish a young, flighty thing who might have trouble adapting, who might suffer from homesickness.

I will suffer from homesickness. I may as well admit it to myself, Isabel thought. *I have never left Boston in my life, except for an occasional trip to the seashore and one autumn jaunt, with a group of teachers, into the bright wooded hills of Vermont.*

That's all right, she told herself sternly. *It's about time for some sort of challenge in your life, Isa. Do not shy away from it, just because you're afraid.*

As she wrote, the thought came to her to send the letter ahead by fast post; it would take several days to compile the other materials. This way Mr. Hay would be aware of her as quickly as possible and on the lookout for the packet which would be following.

With this determination, Isabel copied her first draft onto a sheet of fine writing paper, addressed it, and left it with the librarian to post first thing in the morning with her own outgoing mail.

She felt a bit empty and vulnerable when she walked out of the building, as though she had sent off a piece of her innermost self molded into the simple words.

Do not be so dramatic, Isabel! That is what Aunt Gwendolyn always said. She never thought of herself as dramatic, except perhaps inside her own head—the one private sanctuary where her soul could relax and express itself without fear of censure, without critical eyes watching and judging every free-born thought or urge.

She stepped out into the night. She could smell the sea, though she was miles from the harbor. But a fresh breeze was streaming inland, pushing the bad airs of the day before it. Isabel lifted her face to its caress and could not help noticing the sets of couples strolling aimlessly along the narrow brick walkways, enjoying the soft evening together. *Together. Why did no lone figure walk here, to make her feel less left out, less solitary?*

I must away! I must away, she determined, *before something inside me goes hard. Hard and bitter—and I begin to resemble Aunt Gwendolyn.* The thought made her shudder. She held her head high and walked quickly, but none of the people she passed took any note of her, wrapped up in the sense and presence of one another as they were.

The days passed. Isabel went forward as though all had been decided. She purchased a good, sensible traveling dress of dark color, and warm, sturdy walking shoes. She laundered and mended what she called her "school dresses"—a rational assortment of muslin or linen dresses and rather tailored wool skirts. She next determined what things she absolutely must take with her and what she would be able to part with and leave behind. It was not as though she possessed very much to speak of: her clothes, a modest assortment of costume jewelry, a fair collection of books—but most of those she would pack up to be stored in the attic—a few pieces of bric-a-brac collected through the years, and several framed prints (some clipped out of magazines and catalogs) which she would very much like to make room to bring. The furniture belonged to Aunt Gwenie: the bed Isa slept in, which had also been used by her mother, she would miss, as well as the low, spindle-backed rocker where her mother used to sit and hold her when she was a child. She remembered so little! Try as she would, there were many blank, gray sheets between the few bright pictures her mind possessed.

"Your mother's death was a trauma to you, a tragedy too much for your young mind to accept, so you shut it out." That was Aunt Gwen's explanation. Isabel knew it was partly true. But not altogether . . . and, whatever the cause, she lamented the impoverishment that had resulted, and resented her aunt for refusing to furnish more, when she so easily could.

In the early years it had been: "You are too young to understand, dear, and it is yet too painful for me to discuss, Isabel. Someday, when you are grown." Isabel waited. At length the excuse became altered, turning back upon itself. "That was all so long ago, Isabel. Why talk of the past now? Both your parents are gone. Dragging them out of the shadows and dusting off their memories won't bring them back again." At this point, Aunt Gwen would wrinkle her nose in distaste. "You may uncover things that are better left hidden. No. I cannot answer your questions, Isabel."

And so it had been. And there was no one else. Gwen and her mother at one time had two brothers, but one had died as a lad, one as a young man, leaving no wife or children behind. "Nothing but the two of us," Aunt Gwen liked to remind her. "A maiden aunt and—" She would raise her eyebrows at Isabel and shrug her shoulders. "Well, your life, dear, remains to be seen." That was all, save for the clear implication behind the words: *But I do not think it promises much.* "Pity if the Jonathan Emerson line should die out with us, dear."

Isabel despised such conversation. Once when she was young and feeling particularly plucky she countered, "It should die out with you, Aunt, not me. My name is really Sinclair."

Gwendolyn had turned upon Isa with a fierceness that had startled her. "Sinclair was your father's name, Isabel. Your mother chose to give you her name. An honorable name is a legacy you should not scoff at nor take lightly, foolish girl!"

"Why do you hate my father?" Isabel had demanded. But Aunt Gwen shut up as tight as a clam, and she could get nothing more from her. "I don't hate him," Isa had cried. "I remember him tickling me under the chin and laughing. I remember him singing to me. I remember . . ."

Aunt Gwen had marched from the room at that point, thin lips stretched tight, eyes blazing. And Isabel had stumbled up the stairs, thrown herself onto her bed, and cried.

So the days passed. And so the memories dimmed, in a present which would give them no place.

Hopeful, despite her own inner voices urging caution, Isabel sent off the precious letters and records which comprised the whole of her life. *This is the sum total of what I am,* she thought. *What else have I contributed? I have no religion to which I devote myself, no children of my own, no people who need me, no brilliant accomplishments. I merely point the way and watch other people's lives flow around me.*

She knew she was feeling sorry for herself. Yet that hope, that odd sense of anticipation, roused itself despite her, and would give her no peace. She continued to plan, she continued to prepare for a future that existed, so far, in her expectations alone.

In Boston the Fourth of July is perhaps the most important day of the year. It is celebrated with pride and abandon: parades and fancy speeches, concerts on the Common, circuses, contests, fashion shows, boat races, and fireworks. Isabel watched, as if from a distance, somehow already detached from the exuberance that exploded around her. *I am leaving,* she thought, with an odd sense of clarity. *I may not return to this city for a long time, for years. My last Fourth of July . . . my last summer walking the Common . . . the colors of autumn will quicken and blaze without me, and life will go on, as though my life, the light impression I have made here, had never been. If I had someone,* she mused, *someone with whom to rejoice, to celebrate . . .*

One cannot be jilted in love without expecting some consequences, some serious reactions. Isabel understood that and tried to be patient with herself while she waited, while she checked the daily mail with a painful heartbeat and spent long moments every night kneeling on the braided rug beside her four-poster bed in deep, earnest prayer.

July had not yet relinquished her languid, bee-sweet hours when Isa's reply, in an unexpected form, arrived. As luck would have it, Aunt Gwendolyn went to the door and signed her name for the telegram before the uniformed delivery boy would hand it over to her. She drew herself up in her usual manner, but for some reason Isabel was not afraid of her. She snatched the thin, yellow sheet from her outstretched hand.

"Yes, it is for me, Aunt."

"Who in the world could be sending you telegrams?"

Isabel did not want her to know, to taint her secret world that had thus far been kept safe from intrusion. She smiled a bit thinly. "I believe I shall read this in my room," she said, turning her back on any reply that might be forthcoming and racing up the stairs with a lamentable lack of dignity. But that could not be helped. She shut the door behind her and slit the seal with trembling fingers, then drew the yellow sheet out. The sparse words leapt out at her.

Application accepted. Delighted. Expect you by 29 September. Will reimburse passage fare. Details will follow. P. J. Hay

Isa sank onto the edge of her bed, too stunned to think, to react. *It is done*, she thought dimly. *Did I ever really believe it would happen?*

She expected to be afraid, or overjoyed; she was neither. A calm as rich as the afternoon sun settled over her. *I had better go purchase my ticket*, she thought, and smiled, surprised at herself.

She put on hat and gloves and tucked the telegram into her pocketbook. What should she tell Aunt Gwendolyn? The words came of their own accord, as she descended the stairs under the force of that iron gaze.

"I have accepted a teaching position away from Boston, Aunt."

"Away? What in the world do you mean, girl? Have you taken leave of your senses? I want the details at once."

"If you had only not demanded them!" Isa replied. "I shall tell you in good time, Aunt. Right now I have some errands I must see to at once."

She slipped past the stark, shocked figure and into the open security of the street, where she knew her aunt would not follow. She
felt, not as though her future was opening up before her, but rather
that she was living her life for the very first time.

❧ *Chapter Three* ❧

T HE *FLYING CLOUD* WAS NOT A NEW SHIP, but she was a clipper, with six rows of sails to a mast, built right here in East Boston at Donald McKay's shipyard. McKay, as everyone knew, was the finest designer of clipper ships in the world.

Isabel was pleased to have secured a berth on her, even though she would be sharing the cramped cabin with another female passenger who, up to the time of sailing, would be a stranger to her. The agent at the ticket office told Isa it would take nearly a month to cross the Atlantic—half again as much for the return westward journey, as the ship would be bucking the strong westerly gales.

"I shall not be making the return crossing," she told him.

"One-way ticket then, miss?"

"For the time being, yes, thank you."

For the time being . . . for the time being . . . the phrase stuck in her head. *That is all any of us has,* she reasoned, *the time being, the moment.* It felt good to be using it, to make something happen, rather than to sit placid and passive while life passed her by.

When she told Aunt Gwen that she was taking a teaching position in England, her long rigid face grew pale. "I would not advise it, Isabel, I would not advise it. Such a long way from home. And there are temptations—snares you are not even aware of."

Isabel held up her hand. "I will hear nothing of your dire predictions and gloomy advice, Aunt. I have made my decision and acted upon it. I have a cabin on the *Flying Cloud,* and we sail on the nineteenth of August—and you cannot change my mind."

A strange sort of truce developed between them of necessity. Still reluctant, Isabel did not give her aunt an address. "I do not know where I shall be living," she hedged, though the statement was true enough.

"The school? Surely you have an address for the school."

"I do not. I shall write to you once I've arrived, Aunt Gwen, and am settled in."

Gwendolyn believed her young niece had taken leave of her senses, so the distress she exhibited was real enough. Yet concern, genuine concern, for her welfare—Isabel never felt that. She longed for someone with whom to share her excitement. She missed the intimacy she had become accustomed to these last months with Lawrence. The few female friends she might call close were all teachers like herself, and they tended to lose contact with one another during the summer months. *Solitary*. The word kept surfacing in her mind. *I am a solitary person removing to a solitary part of England to live out my insignificant life.* She could laugh at herself when her thoughts became dismal like this. But she was lonely, and she longed for someone to bless, or at least encourage, her along this new, uncertain path.

The day arrived, as all days in their course do. Isa had sent for a cab and then gone into the parlor where her aunt sat with a basket of mending. She dreaded the prospect of bursting into tears and was relieved to be able to bend over and kiss the wrinkled cheek with no display of emotion. "Take care of yourself while I am gone."

Aunt Gwen sniffed disapprovingly and peered over the top of her glasses. "I could say likewise to you, and much more, but you will not hear me."

Isabel straightened herself with a sigh. "You could also say, 'I love you, Isabel, go with God's blessings and mine.'"

"I could not say that!"

"No, you could not." Isa had already turned away, overcome suddenly with a sorrow that threatened to engulf her. *Is this how my father felt?* she thought, unaccountably, *when he walked away from me and my mother those long years ago?*

She let herself out the front door and down the steps to the waiting taxi. She did not look back. Every inch of the old house, the old neighborhood, existed in her memory; every bit of her life up to this point, good and bad, went with her. She could not have dislodged any piece of it, even if she had wanted to.

Shipboard life was a world of its own, and four weeks of days can be a long time when spent in one place among an odd assortment of people from whom one cannot escape.

Isabel's cabin mate, Julia Morrison, was a young girl of nineteen who was going across to join her mother and sisters in London. She was pleasant enough, but too pretty and vivacious to sit still for a minute, and she did not wait for Isabel to come tagging behind. The social whirl—from the bon voyage party to the card games, costume balls, and cocktails in the salons—became the objects of her enthusiasm from early in the morning until the wee hours of night. Isabel left her alone, preferring the more quiet pursuits of a brisk walk along deck in the morning, a luxurious hour or two spent on a lounge chair with a friendly book and a cup of beef tea, small sandwiches and cakes midafternoon, and evenings spent in the conservatory where modest concerts were performed for the less lively passengers. It all seemed like heaven to her. She had not suffered much from sea sickness, save for a terribly green, queazy, light-headed feeling which disappeared after the first few days. She enjoyed watching the rich women sweep past in their morning promenade costumes, fashioned of mixed wool and silk in various subdued colors with poplinette collars, shoulder epaulets with navy braid and tiny brass buttons, or narrow waists adorned with ribbon girdles tied in knots and falling in long ends over their elegant skirts. Evening gowns were of brocaded satin or taffeta chine, creamy shades of yellow, cool shades of green or porcelain blue, with more roses and lace and embroidered white silks than Isa had ever seen.

We are a stolid lot in New England, she concluded, somewhat overwhelmed by the opulence and excess around her. She was amused, despite herself, at the older passengers, sedate and dignified, who constituted the majority of her companions at the musical recitals. She did not mind. She was doing what delighted her: reading, writing, watching people . . . looking out to sea, where the waves surged and fell, as infallible as eternity, and their very certainty cheered her with the beautiful conviction that the world, and all about it, was in caring and competent hands. When the boat docked at Liverpool, she was not only rested, but the rags and tatters of her old life, which she had wrapped so carefully round her, had been blown to shreds by the sun and the sea winds. She felt fresh and alive, in some sense born anew.

No one knows me in England, she thought, as she followed the press of bodies down the covered gangplank. *I can begin all over again. Nothing will be considered a surprise, nothing will be questioned. I can make of myself whatever I desire to be.*

It was cold. The dampness sat in her hair, clung to her skirts, and wilted the stiff press of her collar. She had been off the ship for six hours now, and the ground was still reeling beneath her. But she had found her way to the rail depot and discovered that there was one last evening train leaving for the north. She would rather be on it than spend the night in a rented room in Liverpool. Here in the business district, the city was a bit overwhelming: dirty, noisy, and crowded, with too many strange men who glanced askance at her; a young woman alone. Isabel shivered and thrust her gloved fingers into the pockets of her black beaver cloak, wishing she had given in and purchased the long fur coat she had eyed and resisted all last winter.

"Train should be here any moment, miss." The gentleman waiting beside her grinned encouragement and Isa gave him, in return, as bright a smile as she could muster. He was a man in his midsixties and appeared respectable and safe enough.

"There'll be hot tea on the train, that'll cheer you," her companion predicted genially. "You be going all the way into Scotland?"

"I'm getting off at Haworth."

"Haworth and the moors for you then, is it?"

"I am going to teach there."

"I say! Teachers come younger and prettier every day, miss." To Isabel's amazement, the man winked and tipped his hat to her, and as the train chugged into the station, he waited to hand her up, then carry her bags and deposit them safely in the racks above her.

She settled into her seat with a sigh. Liverpool to Yorkshire was a considerable distance, probably over 150 miles as the tracks ran. At nearly 90 kilometers, or 50 miles an hour, that meant the journey would take 3 hours or more, plus time for stopping and starting.

Once she had checked with the station master and obtained this information, she had spent the money to send a telegram to inform Mr. Hay, and could now only hope that someone would be at the village station to meet her. At 9:30 p.m. on a September evening in Haworth, would all the folk be in bed?

There was still light enough to see by, the silty gray glimmer of evening, with all the sunshine washed out. Isabel pressed her nose to the window and watched the green fields of England stream past her. Liverpool to Manchester, then Leeds, where industry had scarred the landscape and pushed back the gentle curves of farm and fell. As they approached North Yorkshire, the moorlands opened up before them; a stark, unlit landscape, smeared with dark plum-shaded bruises, dotted with villages half swallowed in folded valleys, punctuated by craggy ruins rising haphazardly above the barrenness, empty and silent against the pearled stretch of sky. And in the distance the backbone of England, the Pennines, ran ever northward, as though racing the night.

The rawness of the scene smote Isabel forcefully; she felt something within her recoil from the sight. Yet, at the same time, she was drawn with an almost macabre fascination, and she trembled as the conflicting emotions jarred through her.

From Leeds the train rumbled through Bradford, five miles further to Thornton, Denholme, then up a black stretch of moor into Haworth. Isabel realized with a start that her journey had ended. The train stood snorting and breathless as a horse reined to a stop. She stood and stretched, and looked about her; it seemed there were no other passengers making preparations to disembark here. She stood on tiptoe attempting to pull down her portmanteau and satchel from the upper compartment when she sensed, rather than heard, the approach of another person behind her.

"Miss Emerson, is it? Might I be of assistance?"

The voice had the refined modulations of a gentleman. Isabel turned. "P.J. Hay at your service, miss. So glad you've safely arrived."

"As am I!" Isa breathed. She liked the look of this man. He must be seventy, or approaching it; she had not expected that. He was thin as a rail, shoulders rounded and head bent a little, as though it would hurt him to stand upright. His deep-set eyes were patient and tired, yet they conveyed a subtle spark, as did his quite ordinary voice.

"My trap is waiting," Mr. Hay said, as he lifted down her belongings, "and we are only minutes from home. Bertha, my housekeeper, will pour you a cup of hot tea and see to your needs, my dear."

He began to pad down the aisle, so Isabel followed, feeling suddenly tired and a little bleary-eyed. There was so much she was curious about, so much she wanted to ask. As if privy to her thoughts, Peter Hay patted her hand as he lifted her up to her seat. "Time enough tomorrow to ask questions. Time is the one commodity we have in abundance here, I can assure you. Right now you need to settle into the nice bed Bertha has prepared for you and get a decent night's sleep."

That is precisely what she did. Bertha, as sparse of person as her employer, led her to an upstairs apartment that was roomy and furnished with large, ornate furniture, much of it darkened by age. But the fire in the grate and the steaming cup by her bedside rendered the room cozy. She did not even unpack. Bertha undid her stays, unbuttoned her shoes, and pulled a cool white muslin sleeping gown over her head. She relaxed against the down mattress gratefully, taking a long sip of the hot, comforting liquid before closing her eyes, and was not even aware when sleep stole over her, as gently as the clouds that sat lightly on the horizon and obscured the low hills.

❧ Chapter Four ❧

"ARE YORKSHIRE BREAKFASTS CUSTOMARILY so hearty?" Isabel asked, standing with her plate by the sideboard, wondering which food to sample first.

"A day or two of this bracing air and you'll notice a change in your appetite," Bertha assured her.

Isa helped herself to a modest sampling of eggs, sausage, thick-sliced ham, and a porridge both stiff and creamy, which she drowned in a generous portion of cream. But she ate only sparingly, sitting alone at the broad dining room table while Bertha bustled about.

"Mr. Hay will be home directly, miss. You're to make yourself comfortable until his return." She began to turn back to her work, then remembered and added, "If you'd like to go to meeting with the master, he said he would be pleased of your company."

"What time do services begin, Bertha?"

"Straight up noon, miss. Two hours from now."

She had slept late! But at least she felt rested, if a bit disoriented. She climbed the stairs and returned to her room where a small hip bath sat on the tiled floor beside the fireplace, filled with warm water. Bless Bertha! This was just what she needed. Then to the parish church with the professor. She was looking forward to that.

The past is more real here than the present, Isabel thought. *It sounds in the wind and thickens the air we breathe.* She would like to have said so to Mr. Hay, who had linked his arm through hers, but did not feel she knew him well enough yet.

The morning mists had burned off, but the day remained gray, and the gloomy sky pressed like a ceiling upon the stony village that clung to the moor with the tenacity of the gorse and heather, which the harsh howling winds of countless bitter winters could not dislodge. *Do others feel it,* Isabel wondered, *the same way I do?*

She followed Mr. Hay to his family pew and they sat down, the only two on the cold bench. But all eyes turned their way. Isa thought of the service she had attended in Boston and the inquisitive eyes that had bored into her then. She felt an urge to turn round and smile at the curious villagers, who doubtless wondered about the stranger and what she would bring to this place—this quiet place that had belonged to them and theirs for generations—and desired nothing but continued isolation and peace. She understood, so much more than they realized.

"My dear."

She turned to see Mr. Hay's gaze fixed thoughtfully upon her. "You look so familiar to me."

"I do not know how that could be."

"Have you ever visited this part of England as a tourist?"

She shook her head. "Have you been to Boston, sir?"

He returned the gesture. "A very fine city, however, from what I have heard."

"I do believe you would like it."

"Oh, yes. Did you know my wife came from Boston? Lived all her young life on Revere Street within walking distance of the Common."

"I know it well!" Isabel could not keep the excitement from her voice. "I had no idea. You did not . . ."

Mr. Hay put a finger to his lips. The vicar and his curate had entered, and their conversation must wait.

So, that is why he advertised in Boston, that is why he wanted an American teacher. This added element excited and pleased her. She could not wait to learn what Mr. Hay's Bostonian wife had been like.

The service seemed tedious, nothing out of the ordinary about it. But, perhaps that was because Isabel, herself, was not in a proper state to sit still. A restlessness possessed her spirit; she had scarcely seen any of Haworth yet, and had met no one but Mr. Hay and his servant. The broad sky and the rising moors were calling her, as if with an audible voice.

But at the end of meeting, their progress from the building was of necessity a slow one. People paused to greet the old gentleman; then, of course, they must be introduced to his visitor—the new teacher he had engaged. Most of the parishioners greeted her warmly enough, but not one asked a question or showed the slightest interest beyond the requirements of propriety. Perhaps it was too soon for that.

Once out of doors the damp tendrils of air wrapped themselves round her. She shook her head as if to dislodge them and had directed her steps toward the graveyard, feeling a pleasant sense of freedom, when she glanced back to see that her companion had been detained and was talking intently with two other gentlemen near his own age.

"Do not hurry," she murmured. "Do not seek me too soon."

The tall leaning grave markers rose before her like a wasteland of stone, frozen at disordered, precarious angles that no human judgment would set. She wove her way among them, stopping here and there to read an inscription, to admire the carved face of an angel or the graceful lines of a cross. A brisk wind accompanied her, nipping at her heels like a bad-tempered terrier, as cold and restless as she.

The image of her mother's grave, an ocean away, rose up to crowd out the others. On a green, sunny slope of the Old Granary her mother rested, protected from the onslaught of the elements by an overhanging canopy of low branches, laden with leaves. When she visited her mother's grave she felt only a vague, gentle sadness, as soft as the sifting sunlight. *Jean Emerson.* The name *Sinclair* had not even been carved into the headstone. Isabel stood thinking upon this strange, unkind fact. Here, where the emotions of the dead seemed violent still, despite the grave's attempts to muffle them, the effrontery of her aunt's actions seemed cruel indeed. Here death remained a shadow, a fleshless stalker whose greedy gaze ever rested upon the living. Isabel felt this strongly—or did her imagination and the black branches dripping upon the leaden landscape only suggest such thoughts?

I do not even know where my father is buried. The realization gave her a start. It had never mattered that much before. He had always been lost to her; the memories she had of him vague and shadowy, part of her little-girl world which she could only dimly recall. Suddenly the huge blank in her mind distressed her. *Where in the world is he? Where?* she agonized. *Where did he die?*

Isabel stood still, feeling the rain like mist, or tears, on her face. When she heard footsteps, she thought it was only the old professor and turned to see. Half-concealed behind a tree a man stood with his head cocked, looking at her—looking at her so intently that she felt his gaze, as surely as if he had reached out and touched her skin.

"I know you," he said.

Or did he? The words sounded strange and garbled. Had she really heard him correctly? He was a middle-aged man. But he wore no hat, and his disheveled hair sat like a mottled cap on his head. There was something simple and childlike in his eyes and the way he would not stop staring. With a shudder she turned away from him and called out loudly, "I am over here, Mr. Hay. Are you ready to leave yet?"

"Are you, my dear?" He approached her from around the side of the parsonage, and an instant relief flooded through her. "I did not wish to disturb your reverie."

She half-turned and cast her eyes to the tree where the strange man had been standing. He was no longer there. Nor could she see him moving along any of the pathways; he had seemed to suddenly disappear.

"You look cold, Miss Emerson. You are not accustomed to our climate yet. Let us get you back to the fire and a cup of hot tea."

Isabel took his arm gratefully. "The spirit is strong in this place," she said.

"You feel it as few do," he replied. And he spoke the words thoughtfully, with his eyes on her face. "It is not merely the tragic, romantic story of the Brontës who lived and suffered here, and thus immortalized the spot."

"No. There is something more, something they knew and understood that existed long before them, that has not perished because they have died."

"The spirit of the land," Peter Hay mused. "The unknown generations of men and women who lived out their lives here—who laughed and cried, who married and gave birth, and passed into the earth again, but did not really die."

"That may be it! I feel the press of their spirits upon mine, as though they are here still!"

"In some ways, they are."

"But why is the sensation so powerful in this place?"

Mr. Hay shrugged his thin shoulders in a gesture of resignation. "That we are not given to know. But there is a reason why you feel it . . . there has to be a reason why such sensations are felt strongly here."

He spoke the words as if he were pleased. *Strange,* Isabel thought. *As strange a beginning to my sojourn here as any I might have tried to imagine.*

She returned to the house with her host and ate a heavy dinner of roast beef and Yorkshire pudding. The rooms of the old place were damp, and there was a lonely air about them, which the bright fire and the kind hospitality could not displace.

"Yes, this is a lonely place," Peter Hay said, and Isabel realized he had been watching her. "There is not much I can do about it." He shrugged his shoulders again in tired resignation. "It has been like this ever since Edith died."

"I am sorry," Isabel said, meaning it. "I do not understand your pain. But both of my parents died when I was a child. I do know what loss is."

"Yes." Again he spoke the word with some kind of pleasure. "That knowledge shows in your face, rare for one as young as yourself." He leaned back in his chair and began to shake out his pipe. "I was fortunate in my selection of a teacher this time, wasn't I?"

"Have you had American teachers before?"

"Oh, yes. In the village they all laugh and make fun of me, but I mind it not; people must have something to talk about." The patient eyes sparkled. "I've been up to such nonsense these thirty years— ever since I lost her. I thought new blood and an outside perspective would be good for us. I own the school, you see, and can do as I like with it."

"Has it worked out all right, then?"

"Sometimes yes, sometimes no. At first I was indiscriminate: man or woman, no specific age, no requirements beyond the obvious qualifications. But the men did not work out at all."

Isabel smiled. "And why is that?"

"Different reasons each time, so it's hard to say. But they did not seem to adapt as well, nor accept our ways and our customs with the same understanding the women showed."

Isabel arched an eyebrow. "I'm not surprised."

Peter Hay chuckled. "Yes, the women do have something about them, some inner strengths and insights we men are not privy to. You'll get no arguments from me on that count."

"How did she die, your Edith?"

"Consumption."

"That is how my mother died."

"It is a terrible, terrible thing."

"I was nearly eight years old when she died, but I seem to have shut out so many of the memories." Isabel realized that her voice was trembling; she put her hand to her mouth.

"You have some, to be sure—the good and gentle ones."

She nodded.

"Let the others rest where they lie, child. They can be of no use to you now."

They sat in silence for a moment. Then Peter Hay sighed and leaned forward a bit, stretching his long legs toward the fire. "Do you remember what Byron said on the subject of dying?"

She was not certain to what the old gentleman referred, but he answered himself. " 'Heaven grants its favorites early death.' So Byron wrote and believed. Strange that he—and many of his best friends—died young themselves."

A shudder ran along Isabel's skin and she pulled her shawl tighter. "Yes, it is strange," she agreed.

"Ah, much about life is annoyingly inexplicable." Peter Hay's laugh was as kindly as his smile. "I do know one thing for certain. I need the long life I've had—my full three score and ten years—if I'm to sneak under the wire and make it to where Edith waits."

Isabel felt the sting of tears in her eyes. She rose, resisting the urge to bend over and kiss the white head. He glanced up. "Be you off to your room then?"

She hesitated. "Are you sure it's convenient? I feel spoiled having my own suite, both bedroom and sitting room."

"Nonsense. You are more than welcome, my dear. 'Tis a pity to have them unused and wasted. Bertha has her room off the kitchen, and I make do splendidly down here." He sought her eyes and the benign smile flickered. "I really cannot manage the stairs."

"All right, then. I shall try to enjoy the luxury. Good night, sir."

The rooms he had given to her really were lovely. Unlike the rest of the house, the furnishings here were offset by what Isa was certain were feminine touches: lace curtains at the windows; striped coverlets over bed and dressing table; well-framed prints of women and children, country gardens and cottages. A miniature enameled clock sat on the mantle, painted with pansies and bluebells in delicate shades. And on the table beside the bed was a leather-bound Bible. Isabel picked it up gently, enjoying the cool weight of it in her hands.

"These were her things, weren't they?" she asked the solemn-faced Bertha, who had glided into the room through the half-open door.

"Yes, they were, miss. Kept much as she left them these many years. Master takes some pleasure in that."

"I can see that he would. It is a pity that he loved her so deeply."

"A pity, miss? Love?"

"No, not love, Bertha. I meant the loss."

"Oh, aye. He hasn't made the least attempt to forget her, the way most folk do."

"Were you here then—did you know her, Bertha?"

"Mistress Edith? From the day she entered this house as his bride, miss. I was a lass of fifteen myself, and proud I were to be serving her."

"How long? I suppose there were not any children?"

"They had but five years together. Miss Edith was never very strong. The last year she spent mostly in bed—right here." Bertha gazed placidly at the high poster bed. Isabel felt her heart constrict. "Is this where she died?"

Bertha nodded, stolidly unaware of the distress her acknowledgment was causing. "In this very bed. Died in her sleep. Peaceful-like, with him holding her hand and stroking it. We all were most grateful for that; for his sake, mind you, as much as for hers."

Isabel swallowed and nodded. She had half a dozen other questions she had been eager to ask, but they seemed suddenly insignificant.

"Like a hot water bottle to warm the sheets, miss, b'fore I turn in?"

"No, but thank you just the same, Bertha."

"All right then. Sleep well, miss. Breakfast at seven."

Isabel nodded. "See you in the morning." She shut the door gently. So Edith Hay died in this room—in the very bed where she had curled up so comfortably.

What of it! she told herself firmly. *Don't tell me you are going to let that fact frighten you?* She sat down on the edge of the plump eiderdown and ran her hand over the faded cloth. Suddenly she was home, sitting on the bed she had slept in since childhood . . . the bed where her mother had died.

What perverse fate places me in such situations? she fumed. She felt suddenly tired—weary. Perhaps she would go to sleep now and face the task of unpacking her belongings and airing her clothes in the morning, when there would be light and fresh air to her convenience.

She let her dress slip to the floor and undid the stays of her corset, breathing freely again. *I was never afraid in my mother's bed,* she thought, remembering. *Instead I felt comforted, somehow closer to her in that place than anywhere else.*

It should not be any different, she reasoned, *with what remains of the spirit of this gentle Edith, who died young and childless and left a grieving husband behind.*

Life and death—where does one state cease and the other begin?

Isabel wondered, convinced that the very air of the ancient, brooding moorlands conceived and nurtured such searchings within the depths of all restless and earthbound souls.

❧ *Chapter Five* ❧

THE MORNING WAS BLESSEDLY MILD; NOT much sunshine, but no rain to dampen both clothes and spirits. Isabel unpacked her belongings, fitting them in, with an odd feeling, among Edith's possessions. She shook out her dresses and skirts and then brushed them thoroughly, opening one of the back windows wide so that the clean air pouring into the room might freshen them.

Her necessary labors completed, she donned warm gloves and hat and headed out to explore the town, this dour spot of earth where fortune had cast her.

Haworth, as Charlotte Brontë herself had said, was ringed with mills as well as moors. The harsh land was not rendered more palatable by the scars left by mills, quarries, and even old open-cast coal mines—ragged, gaping holes forever bereft of green. Peter Hay had told her that the main street of Haworth was reputed to be the steepest street in all of England. The brick and stone of the buildings running into the cobbled stones of the roadway created a dark, almost surly aspect, even on pleasant days. Isabel took it all the way down to where it curved to merge with Bridgehouse Lane, a little above the beck that bore the same name. She could hear the running water of the stream; the sound, beneath the gathering gray clouds overhead, was cold.

She retraced her steps past the row of shops which appeared as though they had stood there for hundreds of years. Their structures were as solid as the rocky flats and hills they grew out of. They housed a meat and vegetable market, a bakery, a blacksmith, a tailor, a shoemaker, a glassblower, and an apothecary. She glanced upon them with interest, but it was the moors she was after, and she began the steep climb above and a little west of the parsonage—set at the very summit of the long narrow street—to the broad open lands beyond. All along the horizon stretched a line of hills, scooped and rounded like waves, fold after distant fold of them. Isabel bent her head, feeling the muscles at the back of her legs tug as she plodded up the rough, rocky incline.

As she climbed she realized that the purple stains she had observed from the train were actually clumps of dark heather, clinging with tough scraggly roots to the uneven soil. The blooms were past their August brightness—they looked dusky and weathered—but they still exuded a heady fragrance, and Isa drew the scented air into her lungs with a sigh.

"I know you! I know you! I seen those eyes watching me yesterday."

Isabel cried out at the sound of the voice with the same alarm as the moor hen, who rose squawking from behind a dip of dry bracken and yellowed grass.

The man ambling toward her took no heed. His shoulders were hunched, and he peered at her from under the brim of a broad felt hat, well-weathered by winds and rain.

"Leave me alone!" Isabel warned. "I do not know you, and you have no right to talk to me." She had nearly said, *You have no right to frighten me*, but caught herself just in time.

"I know you," the voice chimed, innocuous, yet persistent. "I saw you at the churchyard yesterday, remember?"

Isabel shook her head. "Leave me alone," she repeated.

The frumpish man seemed not to have heard her. "I been up above Ponden Hall to Ponden Kirk."

The names meant nothing to Isabel.

"I did see the young ladies from the Parsonage sittin' in the lee of the high stone. I do b'lieve there's a storm blowin' in." He sniffled and wiped his red nose along his shirt sleeve. "I did tell Emily that."

"Emily?" Isa repeated, without thinking.

"Emily. Who do love the moors more than the others." He chuckled to himself, as though some memory had tickled his fancy. "That one does not mind a good soaking if she be caught out alone!"

The speaker hunched his broad, rounded shoulders and looked down at his shoes. "The black clouds scare me, they do."

"Then you had best go on home." Isabel spoke as though to a child, but the strange man stood his ground.

"I b'long here. It's all right. I've got shelters—" he waved his long arms—"all along here." He raised his eyes to hers again. "But there do be a storm coming on."

Isabel realized the implication and thought suddenly that she should return, just in case the stranger spoke right.

With ill grace she turned her back on her visitor who, to her surprise, let her go. For several yards she resisted the urge to pause and glance behind her. When at last she did, there was no sign of him, of any kind of life moving across the moor.

She hurried her pace, because the sky did seem to be lowering, and the air held an eerie stillness that intensified her sense of solitude. Before she could reach the parsonage, the rain broke over her head, sheets of cold water that seemed to instantly soak her. She ducked into the nearest lane and pressed herself against the side of a building under a low-hanging eave where the fingers of the rain could not reach.

She stood there, breathless and shivering, when all at once a feeling of sadness came over her—a sadness so hopeless, so palpable that it sent a shudder of despair all through her. For a moment, as the wind rose, she fancied she heard the sound of voices—low voices, thick with anguish, trembling along the air. She shook her head and realized she was moaning in protest.

I cannot stay here! she thought, overwhelmed by the weight that seemed to come at her from all sides and pull her soul down. She darted out into the gale, bending her head before it, straining on, past the triangle of parsonage, church, and schoolhouse, to the junction where West Lane runs into Main Street, and Mr. Hay's stone house stood waiting.

Bertha saw her from the window and had the door open and waiting as she struggled up the wet stairs.

"Goodness, miss. I was that worried about you! This storm blew up in a hurry, I was afraid you might be caught out on the moors."

Isabel took the rough woolen blanket Bertha handed her and relinquished her soaked hat and cape into the capable hands that carried the sodden mess across to the stone-flagged storage room off the old kitchen where the large laundry tubs stood. Isa removed her dripping dress and scurried up the stairs in her shift to find something warm and dry to put on. *Dismal! Is this what life here will be like?* she despaired. *Everything in this place is dark! The sky, the land, the buildings—even the people!*

She knew this was neither entirely true nor entirely fair. But she could not help wondering what she had gotten herself into by this choice she had made.

Bertha knocked at the door with a cup of steaming tea. "You'll accustom yourself in time, miss," she said by way of comfort. "School starts Thursday-week, and then you'll have something to keep yourself occupied."

"Thursday-week? You mean in two days? I thought the Michaelmas term began in October."

"Generally does. But the headmaster, Bertram Hopkins, has his sister's wedding to go to in London mid-October, so we're beginning the term early and having a bit of a holiday in between! Didn't Mr. Hay tell you?"

We! Isabel thought. *Why should this woman know more of my business than I do?"*

She was in an ill humor because she was wet and cold, even the inside of her mouth tasted musty. There was no place to go and nothing to do—and she could not dislodge the face of the strange man on the moors from her head. *Ought I to mention running into him?* she wondered, but thought better of it. Not now. Not yet. Certainly not to Bertha, despite the fact that Bertha seemed to know just about everything.

"Dreadfully sorry, my dear. You're quite right, I should have told you before."

Isabel sighed at the good professor who sat by the fire cradling his teacup with both hands, his feet propped on the edge of the fender for warmth.

"We have not even discussed curriculum."

"I am sure you have ideas—your own preferences."

"Yes, but . . ."

Mr. Hay waved one hand in a gesture of munificence. "Please yourself, Miss Emerson—please. I have perfect faith in you."

"But . . . ," Isabel's mind was floundering, "are there no requirements? What have the young ladies studied previously?"

"A smattering of English literature through the ages, nothing more. You will have the fourth through sixth form girls, my dear, aged roughly eleven to fourteen; fertile ground, you can see, fertile ground." Peter Hay took a long appreciative sip of the steaming liquid before continuing. "Give them your favorites, the things you are passionate about—that is what I want them to feel!"

Isabel drew in her breath, surprised that her mind was already teeming. "British writers, to be sure, but I should like a good smattering of American authors and poets."

"By all means!" Mr. Hay leaned forward, his own eyes eager. "That is what I brought you here for. We are too narrow in these parts, far too narrow. I can do these young gels a great service by stretching their minds and their abilities to appreciate, don't you think?"

"I do." Isabel held strong opinions of her own on such subjects.

"You have brought along a variety of your own books, as I suggested in my last letter?"

Isabel blinked. "I do not believe your last letter reached me, sir, before I sailed."

"Blast the mails!" he responded.

"Oh, but I have brought such books, anyway; sufficient, I believe, to effect what you have described."

"Excellent!" Mr. Hay nodded and sipped at his tea again. "It is only a small school," he continued, growing reflective. "But enough students pass through it that you and I can hope to make our mark, bring about some real difference here and there. Each heart and mind—think how many countless others it goes on to influence."

"Yes, sir, I agree with you heartily on that score."

"I thought you might." He smiled beautifully. "You see, I mean for you to take your ease—experiment, give yourself latitude—see what is most powerful, what works best."

"A rare luxury for a teacher," Isabel mused aloud.

"A rare luxury for anyone. But, since I own the school outright and do not depend upon its income as a source of sustenance . . ." Hay lifted his eyebrows conspiratorily, as if to say, *Such fun! Aren't we the lucky ones?*

Isabel could have sung out with joy. No longer did she feel over-whelmed, even frightened, but eager.

"Your tea is getting cold, my dear."

Isabel returned from her thoughts with a start. Suddenly she felt ravenously hungry, and the gray day outside was no more than that; poor weather. And of what consequence is poor weather when one has fine, shining challenges and scope for action ahead?

The following day Mr. Hay took Isabel to Stanbury in his trap that she might view the school and get a sense for the layout of the building before classes began. There was little more than a mile sep-arating the two villages, and the ride was pleasant, up toward the high country and the open moors. Moorcrag School was aptly named, for it sat atop a slight eminence and commanded a view of the surrounding hills as well as a broad swath of valley, including the rooftops of Haworth, with the church tower prominent among them. The building was made of gray brick with many wide bowed win-dows, which lent it a light, friendly air. The wide curved steps that led up to it were weathered with age and worn smooth in places from the passage of many feet.

"The place was a school long before I obtained it," Mr. Hay ex-plained. "I could never find out for certain what it was originally built as nearly two hundred years ago. But it has served our purposes well."

Isabel liked the rooms, with their dark wood wainscoting and high ceilings. Along the walls hung a fine assortment of framed por-traits and landscapes, most of them copies, she presumed. "Are the paintings your doing?" she asked Mr. Hay.

"I confess they are, lass. Aspect's so dreary otherwise."

"These people are fortunate to have you."

Peter Hay laughed heartily. "I would not take bets as to how many would agree with you there, my dear."

Isabel sat herself down in the room where she would be teaching, gazing at the tidy rows of desks, trying to picture the faces which would be greeting her in two-day's time.

"We are in luck! Headmaster Hopkins is here making preparations, and I shall be able to introduce you to one another."

Mr. Hay stood in her doorway beaming, so Isabel followed him to the other end of the building into a large, well-appointed office. The man who had risen to stand behind his desk in order to properly greet her was of average height and weight, average coloring, medium age; nothing overt about him to mark him from other men. Even his voice, when he spoke to return her polite pleasantry, was monotone, with no color to it, no sense of life.

He does not like me, Isabel thought at once, sensing the accuracy of the instinctive feeling as it struck her. *Perhaps because I am an American—and being thrust upon him.*

He was cold. Perhaps coldness was his way. Certainly most British men, those in Yorkshire particularly, were reticent and stiff mannered. As the three of them chatted, Isabel did her best to stir some response from this person who would be boss or, as the English put it, governor over her. Nothing. It was as though he were determined to remain detached, even unpleasant.

Isabel escaped from the room with a sense of relief that must have shown on her features. "Not much impressed, eh?" Mr. Hay smiled down on her.

"Let me just say, I should hate to be caught out in some mischief and have to answer before those cold eyes." On impulse she added, "What made you hire that sort of man?"

"Didn't know he was that sort, and didn't have much choice in the matter. I needed a qualified headmaster or mistress and could find none hereabouts, or none who were willing to relocate here. Had to have someone; couldn't shut the school down."

"Are you stuck with him, then?"

Mr Hay chuckled indulgently. "I love the directness of you Americans. No beating about the bush, as you say; no polite fencing."

"To what purpose, sir? Quality will always rise to the surface and ought to have its chance, don't you agree? In America we provide the means for that—the person before the custom, you might say."

"Bravo!" Peter Hay hugged her enthusiastically, leaving her a little flustered. "You're a bit of all right, my girl."

He was pleased with himself for having discovered her, though his good fortune was, in truth, due to the whims of circumstance largely beyond his control. *This enthusiasm of his for things American,* Isabel thought, *is already becoming annoying to me. I can imagine what his English colleagues think of it!*

They drove together the short distance back to Haworth. The sun was quickly disappearing behind the horizon, as though falling suddenly off the very edge of the earth. The long evening stretched before Isabel, but at least she would have work with which to fill it. And the work of the mind was a pleasure to her; she felt a keen appetite for it, and a sense of anticipation for the hours that lay ahead.

⋙ Chapter Six ⋘

THE FOURTH THROUGH SIXTH FORM GIRLS were most proper young English ladies. They sat with hands folded in the laps of their pleated uniform skirts and stared straight ahead at the new teacher, scarcely blinking or showing any flicker of expression. Isabel could not help being amused. *This is much better,* she thought, *than rude, unruly behavior. I am patient; I can deal with this.* Surely they were at least as frightened of her as she was of them. Everything would be a bit new and different to them as well as to herself for a while. After all, a curriculum which included Edgar Allan Poe, Walt Whitman, Emily Dickinson, Washington Irving, and Nathaniel Hawthorne was little short of revolutionary in these girls' eyes.

Her fellow teachers were another thing. They were mildly polite, because they were British. It was a point of pride to display good manners to strangers, especially strangers from the colonies—which is how many of them still referred to Americans. Isabel had the distinct impression that they were weary of their patron's errant behavior and would "put up with" one more American thrust into their midst only because they must.

What did you expect to encounter? Isabel kept asking herself. *You made this decision in haste and expected even the dark aspects of the adventure to be tinted with romance.* It was difficult to admit this to herself, that at heart she was a romantic, even after long years spent in the harsh school of realities. *Can I make a place for myself here?* she wondered. But she realized that only patience and the workings of time could provide an answer to that.

Meanwhile she tried to remember essentials: Arthur Thomas, a corpulent man with massive mutton-chop sideburns, was in charge of the sciences; Frank Martin, quiet in demeanor and soft-spoken, taught mathematics; Morris Dalton, slim and impeccably groomed, with a narrow, intelligent face and a wonderful patrician nose, was instructor of both history and Latin. Did every school, even modest country girls' schools like this one, have a heart throb, one gentleman teacher who set all the girls sighing? Paul Kennedy was the German master, of all things, and he possessed the broad Germanic features: heavy-browed and blue-eyed, with thick curly hair the color of ripened wheat. He taught at several other schools in the area and made his home in York, which lent him the additional attraction of being a stranger from what was considered by these girls a metropolis.

Some of the accents hereabout were thick, and Isabel had difficulty understanding two or three of her students, as well as Violet Massey, the French teacher, and Mr. Thomas. She knew a few of her students had difficulty understanding her, though they were afraid to say so. She tried to remind herself to speak slowly and distinctly, but time after time found herself forgetting in the enthusiasm for her subject.

The school was modest, and Isabel realized at once that her own duties were light: three English classes each day; one to the middle form girls, two to the upper, and an afternoon course Mr. Hay had titled "The Progress of Poetry", subtitled "Exercises in the Discovery of the Human Spirit." Just what she had thought she wanted when she left Boston; now she did not feel sure.

There were only two other women at the school, besides herself: Helen Hunter, who had charge of the lower form students; and Violet Massey, French instructress to all the girls, who also doubled as Helen Hunter's general assistant.

A small group of strangers thrown together. Isabel wanted so much to make something good of it. *Don't try to look too far ahead,* she warned herself. *Take it one day at a time. Feel your way. You cannot see clearly what you do not yet even know.*

The first day went well, and so did the second. She handed out her first assignments to her students. One girl moaned dramatically when told they would be reading Longfellow and Wordsworth and comparing them. But Isabel ignored her entirely. Monday next, with an entire week of classes before them, would tell. For the time being she had two days to herself. There were several of her friends she wished to write, and she ought to write Aunt Gwenie as well, now that something had happened, and she had more than vague impressions and fears to report.

After less than a week with Peter Hay, Isabel was at the point of distraction. The old man was lonely and, without really meaning to, consumed nearly all her spare time. That, in itself, was a source of frustration. But the unbearable part was his propensity for anything and everything American—he asked her hundreds of questions; he wanted to talk about nothing else. There was a comic element to it: Isabel had come away, this far away, in order that she might forget Boston and turn her thoughts and desires to new things. Mr. Hay, feeding his own hunger, simply would not allow this to be.

Perhaps that was why, when Saturday morning dawned fine and cloudless, Isabel abandoned her letter writing for a walk through the village to take another look round. Perhaps she might find someplace else, modest and unobtrusive, where she could lodge, but without hurting Mr. Hay's feelings? What could she do about that?

There was nothing: a few "Rooms to Let" signs, but not one that looked in the least bit appealing. She turned her steps away from the streets of houses and followed along the footpath that ran from the village to the open moors. The way was lined by trees on both sides; a dark, narrow passage, with a stone wall two feet high preventing the encroachment of the trees into the hardened dirt path. It was dark here, even on a sunny day, and could be menacing as well, though this morning Isabel felt only a sense of peace in the stark solitude.

Sheep dotted the far-off grazing fields, dappled beneath the high sun. Closer, the stone-strewn wastes inclined steeply toward Penistone Crags and Crow Hill. Isabel followed one of the many footpaths that veered away to the right, because off in the distance she had spotted what looked like a mammoth and overgrown house, rising out of the brown folds of earth at its feet with the tenacity and starkness of the rock piles that were its only neighbors.

She followed the path and its meanderings for some distance. At the bend of a rather sharp turn she came upon a low, thatched cottage, rather spreading in nature, with a small barn built to the back of it. It was obviously unlived in; naked windows streaked with dirt revealed nothing but empty, unfurnished rooms. The old mansion beyond it appeared even bigger, its time-blackened walls rising in straight, unforgiving lines toward the high vault of sky. The closer she came, the more deserted the place looked. There were no signs of life, nothing moving except the moor wind ruffling the stiff tufts of faded heather that clung in the thin cracks of soil.

Isabel was curious. Who would build a home in such an isolated setting? What kind of people had lived in this place? How long had the brooding, taciturn building been standing here? Just forming the questions in her mind transformed her curiosity into interest—a real desire to know! She walked up the disused, overgrown path toward the neglected house, straight up to the entrance—low and narrow for such a grand place. She paused and forced herself to breathe deeply; then, with both of her hands, gave the door a sharp shove.

The warped wood creaked and moved inward. Isabel put her hand to her mouth and stood undecided a moment. Then, careful as a ghost or a shadow, she slipped inside the narrow opening her own hand had made.

The interior was amazingly light. A wide entrance hall ended at the foot of a broad staircase ahead of her. To her left and her right opened up rooms that were floored with wide planks of wood, cushioned with huge Persian rugs that were dusty and worn. To her left was the parlor, with two French doors flanking a long, elegant fireplace; to her right, then, must be the dining room. She hazarded half a dozen steps further into the interior and saw the table with eight chairs ranked around it and two mammoth, very tarnished candelabra set in the middle.

She shuddered. The air was stale and tasted of dust. She walked cautiously into the dining room, realizing that it led through a high, wide arch into what looked like a sort of music room beyond. She moved closer. The room was small and very richly furnished, with a cherry wood pianoforte sitting against the short inside wall and a violin in a case resting on an ornate marble-top table that occupied the very center of the room.

She moved to the instrument and ran her fingers along the

keyboard; the tuning was off, but the tones were rich and true. She drew her hand back with a start when she realized that the keys were exposed, as though someone had just stood up from playing and walked briefly out of the room. She whirled around, as though she expected someone to accost her. The silence that met her was eerie, unnerving.

I have seen enough for today, she told herself, and hastened to retrace her passage and slip out again into the comparative sanity of the outside world—wild and desolate though it might be.

❧ *Chapter Seven* ❧

I SA MOVED OFF QUICKLY, FEELING A bit ridiculous, as though invisible eyes were watching and mocking her for running away. Running away from what? The silence? Apparitions of her own creating?

She came to a small stone bridge, rising hump-backed and steep above a beck that sang lustily into the dry, colorless soil. A scraggly willow bent thin, drooping branches that trailed in the clear, cold water, turning shiny and black at its touch. A throstle, or song thrush, rose up from the wet stream grasses, its pure, flute-like notes trembling through her so that she paused to listen and sigh.

"It's a sound to set the heart on fire, even in this desolate place, isn't it?"

Isabel jumped at the sound of a voice so near at hand, and was startled to see a man step out from behind a low overhanging of rock, just a few feet ahead.

"A bird does not concern himself with the worthiness of the surroundings that have called forth his song," she answered. "How little like them we humans are."

She saw an expression of interest flicker over the young man's face as he regarded her and was perturbed at how pleased she was to have made a favorable impression.

"You're Peter's American teacher, aren't you?" The stranger was obviously pleased over his discovery. Isabel nodded her head. He continued, "I am Damien Phillips."

"Do you live hereabouts?"

"Occasionally. I was raised in the village; my older brother is vicar there."

"At the church of St. Michael of Brontë fame?"

"The very one."

"How interesting."

"For him, perhaps." Damien Phillips laughed pleasantly. "In truth, Seymour is old enough to be my father; there are twenty-five years between us."

"Yet you are good friends. I can see in your face that you are."

The flicker of interest lit the man's fine features once more. "Yes, we are. Our mother died when I was eleven and Seymour finished the job of raising me, he and Evelyn together."

"Evelyn. His wife?"

Damien Phillips nodded, and Isabel could think of nothing for the moment but the sleekness of his thick golden hair and the fine line of his cheekbones beneath the smiling blue eyes.

"I do not remember meeting her last Sunday when Mr. Hay introduced me to your brother."

"Evelyn died three years ago helping a sick parishioner confined with her sixth child."

"You sound as though you do not approve of the compassion that inadvertently led her to her death."

"If I do not, I have my reasons. She was more than the typical or merely dutiful minister's wife. She gave from the heart, unstintingly."

"How did it happen? Her death, I mean."

"Her horse lost his footing in the mud and rain and her carriage overturned. Broke her neck in the fall; it was really quite dreadful."

"I'm certain it was." Isabel shuddered and turned her eyes away. "It seems the women around these parts die much sooner and in much greater numbers than do the men. I wonder why that is . . ."

"You are a singular thing!" Damien Phillips cried, shaking his head at her. "And, although I know who you are, I do not know your name."

Isabel could feel that her heartbeat had quickened, and it was not an unpleasant sensation. "My name is Isabel Emerson."

"Isabel." He tasted the word on his tongue. "And you come from Boston, if I remember aright."

"Have you ever been to the United States?"

"What in the world would take me there?" the young man cried

42

again, pleasure touching on laughter rich in his voice. "I have been to Italy once, to Paris and the south of France several times." A rueful expression she could not quite take seriously played over his sensitive face. "As you can see, I am not a great traveler, nor can I claim much experience in the ways and wiles of the world."

"Do you wish that you could?"

He regarded both herself and her question carefully for a moment. "Actually, if I must speak truly, I do. I make my living by writing, thus my most valuable textbook is the experiences I have to glean from, and my store is rather scanty thus far."

"I do not believe that." Isabel gazed back at him in turn, and the almost mischievous pleasure danced in his eyes again. "You have experienced more than you will own to. Besides, you have a faculty for spying the gem among the rocks where other eyes would see nothing and pass on by."

"Why do you say such an astounding thing? You do not even know me."

Isabel could feel the heat of a blush creep up her neck to her cheeks. "It does seem a bit forward of me," she admitted, by way of apology. "But your nature seems quite open and expressive. There is some spark of life and inquisitiveness about you that is remarkably contagious."

"That is one of the nicest things anyone has said about me for a long time." Damien inclined his head in an almost gracious gesture. "Thank you, Miss Emerson."

Isabel laughed to cover an uncomfortable sense of embarassment, then asked, in a rather obvious attempt to turn the conversation, "Do you know if anyone lives in that house?"

He raised his eyes to the dark, overbearing edifice. "Not really. It has a strange history. Would you like to hear it?"

"I would. I find myself inexplicably drawn to the place."

Damien's lips pursed in an expression almost of distaste. "You don't say? Well . . . you haven't much company on that count. People hereabouts feel uneasy, some hostile concerning Norman Rucastle, whose cruel pride brought it to this point."

"Rucastle. That is a strange, impressive name. Is he the person who owns the house?"

"No. It belongs to his son." Damien Phillips paused. "Old man Rucastle had two wives, and treated them both quite badly. The first left him, ran away; the second one died. Nasty business. She kept having babies that kept dying. All that was eventually left the old tyrant was his firstborn son, name of Willie John, who had never been quite right in the head."

Isabel felt a little catch in her throat. "This Willie John is . . . around still?"

"Yes, he owns the house, remember?"

"What age is he now?"

Damien's expression softened. "You've run into him, haven't you? I can tell by the look on your face."

"I believe so. I saw him peering at me from behind the stones in the parsonage graveyard. Then the first day I walked up on the moors, he . . . well, he wouldn't leave me alone, he kept babbling—nonsensical things."

"That's Willie John to a tee, my dear."

"*He* owns this grand old house!" Isabel was unabashedly affronted. "He would not know what to do with it—obviously."

"Yes. Well, isn't that how life works?"

Isabel returned the friendly grin. She was somehow sure there was a real sympathy behind it, though Damien Phillips might not admit to it. " 'Stranger than fiction, the truth.' Isn't that what Lord Byron said of it?"

"So he did. I haven't thought of that line for ages, not since prep school."

"And you a writer?"

"Well . . ." The rueful expression again. Did he know the charm it lent his appearance? "If you must know, my writings is of the most dry, uninteresting nature: textbooks and manuals—I even dabble in advertisements."

"It sounds interesting enough to me. There is certainly scope for the original there."

"In adverts, perhaps. But textbooks?" The affronted wrinkling of the nose again.

"Textbooks? Textbooks are often sadly lacking in substance—not to speak of spirit! They ought to incite a curiosity for the subject, an excitement for learning."

Damien nodded thoughtfully. "I'm only teasing you a bit. You spoke my own aims precisely, and spoke them well."

"English history—that is what I took a degree in. I've a chance right now to collaborate on an art history text of Britain. I am rather enthused about that."

"Oh, yes!" *What age is this man?* Isabel wondered. *He must be older than I, despite his youthful air. Has he a wife and children?*

"I'm just here for the weekend," he was saying, "but if I can help you with anything. . . ."

"Actually, you might be able to." She told him of the frustrations she was experiencing living with Mr. Hay and the resentment it occasioned among her colleagues. "I don't know people here, and I want more than a drab room in a second rate boarding house," she concluded, then found herself with unconscious wistfulness gazing toward the empty ruin behind them. "Does this Willie John live there, alone?"

"Of course! There would be room for the both of you to rattle around and not get in one another's way," he teased. "Willie John lives where he pleases. He stays out here when he's a mind to, but never for too long at one spell. I know several old widows in town who take him in when he appeals to them, giving him simple tasks to do in exchange for food and a bed."

"Isn't he capable of more?"

"Not really. If someone had tried to teach him when he was younger . . ."

"What about the gatehouse?" In her excitement Isabel put her hand on the stranger's arm. "It also is empty. Would there be any chance?"

"Of you being able to let it?"

"Does Willie John own it, too?"

"He owns the whole kit and caboodle: both houses and more land than you'd want to hear about. But the vicar has been manager of the estate these past ten years or more."

"Your brother?" Isabel exclaimed. Mr. Phillips nodded.

"Do you think he would help me?"

"This is terribly isolated. Are you certain you would like to be out here?"

"Yes." Again came a sense of anticipation, almost of urgency, which caught Isabel off guard.

"Is it the privacy you are after?" he pressed, watching her with an eye to understanding her.

"It is more possession than privacy," Isabel tried to explain. "I have lived since my early girlhood with a maiden aunt. She brought me up after my parents died. She is very domineering—stifling, really." *Why do I find it so easy to be myself with this man?* "I want something of my own, without having to answer to anyone."

"Then you've come to the right place." There was such sympathy in the voice that Isabel felt herself relaxing. "No wonder Peter has been a trial for you! I'll talk to Seymour myself, prepare the ground a bit, if you'd like."

"Oh, yes. That would be most kind of you."

"My pleasure."

Isabel sighed. "Well, I suppose I had better get back now."

"May I accompany you back to town? If you prefer your privacy, I shall not be offended."

"I would enjoy your company very much, Mr. Phillips."

That radiant, beatific smile again! Damien put out his hand and helped her over a rough stretch, where the road, faint to start with, had been obscured by debris left behind when the high-tide waters of a tempestuous spring had receded. The protruding rocks were sharp and awkwardly strewn, but she could have maneuvered her own way. Yet how nice to lean upon the young gentleman's arm and feel the sinewy strength of it beneath her fingers, be sensible of the closeness of his person—their shoulders touching, his other arm briefly around her shoulders to steady her as they executed a path.

It was too good, too enjoyable. Isabel had not realized how much she missed it during these months after her hopes of such companionship had been abruptly snatched away from her. *Damien Phillips.* A very British name. She had not found most British men to be particularly attractive. She had never in her life had any sort of relationship with a man who was physically beautiful. Why was this one so handsome that it left her weak just to look at him—just to have his blue eyes gaze into hers?

Damien was true to his word. The following day Seymour Phillips sought her out, as soon as the service was ended. "My brother tells me you may have need of my services."

Seymour was similar to Damien in the same gentle deference in manner, even in some of the light, natural charm, unconsciously applied. The vicar's features upon closer perusal were more compact than his brother's: the nose a bit narrower, the gray eyes smaller and not as deeply set, and the coloring sandy. He possessed none of the rich shadings of hair and eye, even of skin tone, which the youngest son had inherited.

Isabel smiled gratefully and followed him into his office that she might better explain. It pleased her to see Damien come up from nowhere and follow them into the room. She had not seen him since the previous afternoon and was not even certain that he had attended the service. Now it was as though a portion of sunlight, warm and golden, had entered the dim enclosure with them. *How are some people,* she marveled, *able to manage that?*

"Damien has explained your reasons for wanting to let the empty gatekeeper's house, Miss Emerson," the vicar began. "And I believe I understand and, at least in theory, approve."

"At least in theory?"

"You would be terribly isolated out there, my dear. What about when the winter storms come?"

"If they prevent me passage, then shall they not prevent the teachers and students passage to Mr. Hay's school as well?"

"Point well taken!" Damien grinned across the room at her. "I have a distinct feeling, Brother, that Miss Emerson is well able to take care of herself."

Seymour Phillips ignored the bantering comment, anxious to press on and logically treat the vital issues at hand.

"Besides, I shall be scarcely half a mile off Mr. Hay's course when he drives to school every morning. He can collect me on his way, sir, if he would be so inclined to do me the service."

She was pleased because she had thought of this, and the vicar seemed to concur.

"You must have some means of transportation of your own; I should not leave you alone out there otherwise."

Damien was scowling in thought. "Peter has that little trap of his wife's stored behind the blacksmith's. Do you think he could be cajoled into giving Miss Isabel the loan of it? If so, I believe we could talk Miss Smythe out of her dappled pony. Both would be easy and gentle enough for her to handle."

The vicar nodded agreement, but added, "I think Miss Emerson herself could talk Peter out of his wife's cherished conveyance; I believe the old man is quite fond of her. Neither you nor I would quite do."

So it was agreed that Isabel must do what, after all, was the decent thing and herself approach Mr. Hay with the entire proposition.

"I am so loath to hurt his feelings," she confessed. "He has been most good to me, and I do not wish him to feel as though I am rejecting his kindnesses, as though I no longer enjoy his company."

"All things in moderation," Damien quipped.

Seymour Phillips leaned across and placed his hand comfortingly over hers where it rested on the arm of the chair. "He will understand, my dear, if you are forthright with him."

"If you are yourself," Damien urged. "Be as passionate about your frustrations and needs as you were with me."

Isabel lowered her eyes, a bit put out that the young man had said that. But his brother seemed to pay it no particular mind.

Damien accompanied her out of the building; in fact, he walked with her the entire way to Mr. Hay's house. "I am a bit concerned about you being out on the moors alone," he confessed, "now that I think upon it. Not for any fear of your safety . . ." he hesitated, "but, there are things which can frighten without harming," he said.

"Willie John?"

"Do not let him spook you, Isabel. He ought not be around much with the hard winter coming. He prefers the warmth and cooked food of the town housewives then."

"I will be careful."

"He is a bit repulsive, but he has never hurt anyone."

Isabel was touched at this concern, so freely given. For some reason she couldn't explain she was not frightened at all. Not even hesitant. Her only concern was Mr. Hay's feelings upon the subject, and she would soon know the answer to that.

She parted from her new friend with a reluctance she hoped she was able to largely conceal. Strange. She had known of his existence for scarcely twenty-four hours, yet her life would be less for the lack of association with him.

"I shall come again at the week's end," he promised, "and help with what moving is left and the heavy jobs of unpacking."

"Are you certain? I do not wish to inconvenience you."

"I hope you do. It would be good for me, and you know it." His charm was too palpable. She trembled at the touch of it. "I come most weekends, as it is," he reminded her. "But now I have a special reason for hurrying down here, and that pleases me."

She wanted to watch him walk away, but did not dare. She let herself in the front door just as Bertha was opening it from the other side.

"Tea is ready and waiting," she said. "I thought I heard you out here on the porch."

❧ *Chapter Eight* ❧

I<small>T WAS SILLY, SHE KNEW, BUT IT TOOK</small> Isabel most of the evening to work up the courage to approach Mr. Hay with her plan. When she did, she was amazed at how easy the whole thing was.

"I will miss your company, my dear, certainly you know that. But we can still travel back and forth to school together, as you have suggested. And I believe it is wise. I heard Arthur and Morris complaining about the privilege extended to some and denied others; came upon them unawares—tried to cover their conversation with a lot of red-faced blustering."

He knocked the ashes from his pipe and smiled across the room at her. "I would not willingly add any more disadvantage to your situation than is already inherent in it. I told you in the beginning, remember, how people hereabouts are tired of me and my ways. They put up with this little eccentricity of mine because they have to. You are the natural one for them to take out their frustrations upon."

"I understand that."

"Yes, but shall you be able to deal with it, Isabel?"

"I think so. I want to. I believe I can make a valuable contribution here."

"As do I. But I also want you to be happy here." His voice was kind. And there was ever a gentle note of sadness in it; a patient, accepted melancholy that he could not disguise. Isabel was suddenly very ashamed of the petty excuses she had used to herself, and to others, in order to get her own way. She felt tears sting her eyes and brushed them away with annoyance.

"Do not be distressed, my dear."

"You are so kind to me."

"Are you not accustomed to kindness?"

"Not really. My aunt was very severe with me. Much expectation, much criticism, but little praise."

"Well, you turned out splendidly, despite her."

It was a quiet observation Peter Hay was making, more than a direct response, and it caused Isabel to gaze at him carefully. He had spoken the words with a matter-of-fact conviction which lent them a pleasing credence. "Is that how you see me?" she asked timidly.

The kindly lines around his eyes crinkled as Peter Hay smiled. "I forget how young people doubt themselves. And, of course, you would particularly; while I can discern that the very difficulties and sorrows of your life built a strength of character into you that you might not otherwise have. You had to seek inward for the things of beauty and truth to sustain you, to form the foundation of your existence. That is seldom bad, and in your case it has proven a blessing, my dear." He shrugged his thin rounded shoulders, and suddenly his years hung on him like a threadbare coat: limp, ill-fitting, in need of discarding.

" 'We never know how high we are 'til we are called to rise,' " Isabel quoted softly. "Lines from an Emily Dickinson poem."

"Very appropriate. Listen, you make your plans, my dear, and I shall do all I can to help."

Isabel rose, tears threatening again. And quickly, before her fears checked her, she crossed the distance between them, bent down, and planted a kiss on the bent head where the dark hair was thinning to limp gray strands. Then, lest he stop her and see the tears, she hurried up the stairs to her own room, where she could cry with no eyes to see her—and think over the words of wisdom and affection that he had bestowed upon her, as precious as the most rare, exotic, or costly gift.

Her first full week of school. But now she had so many other concerns to divert her and claim the remainder of her time and attention that the days fairly slid through her hands. And there were surprises following on the heels of surprises.

Monday, when she and Mr. Hay returned to the house on Main Street, tea was not laid as usual, and Bertha was nowhere to be found.

It is just as well, Isabel thought, and changed into a work dress and apron. *I have much to do, and few hours of daylight left in which to work.* She came back down the stairs and hunted through Bertha's kitchen for dusting cloths, cleaning brushes, and solvents, but could find nothing, not even a bucket to fetch water in.

"Mr. Hay," she called out in consternation. "Have you any idea where Bertha keeps her cleaning things?"

"The pot's on the simmer, my dear," he called back. "Come and have tea with me."

She wandered into the parlor where he was setting out biscuits and little frosted tea cakes. "But, sir, I—I have the gatehouse to clean and make ready, and I had hoped to get started tonight."

He waved his hand at her in a gesture of casual dismissal. "Oh, I would suppose Bertha and her compatriots have made quite a dent in that department already. She said if they got going strong she might not make it back in time for tea." He turned and blinked his deep set eyes, wise and quiet as the eyes of an old reptile.

"I don't understand."

"Sit down and I'll pour out, my dear." He filled her cup to the brim before turning to his own. "There is no way you could manage such a task on your own after hours. Bertha and her friends—half a dozen or more, I would guess—were happy to oblige us. They are accustomed to such work, and they are meticulous as old German housewives. All will be spic and span by the time they are through; you can depend on it."

Isabel felt distress mingled with a relief she could not deny. "That is more than generous, both of yourself and them."

"It is what they do best, and what they most enjoy, Isabel; just as teaching and reading and learning are for you."

"But, what of their wages? You must tell me what they will be and allow me to pay them."

"I rather think not." Mr. Hay chuckled. "I have no need of your money, my dear. Keep it for some good purpose of your own." He patted her hand and selected two or three biscuits to put on his plate. "We may have bread and cheese with cold beef if Bertha forgets us much longer," he added with a wink.

"We can certainly manage." Isabel could not help smiling at her friend in return.

Isabel did up the tea things, and when seven o'clock came with no sign of Bertha, she talked Mr. Hay into allowing her use of the kitchen and had potatoes and smelt fried up by the time the weary housekeeper walked in the door. It pleased her to be of some service after all that was being extended in her behalf. Bertha was rosy-faced and cheery, as though hard, back-breaking labor agreed with her.

"Thomas needs to be called, as you suspected, to repair some of the doors and caulk the windows against winter," she told Mr. Hay.

"I'll see to that tomorrow."

"Floorboards are good, very few warped. Plumbing seems in order."

"Are there rugs in any of the rooms?"

"We took 'em up and tossed 'em in the trash bin, sir. A right mess they were, all dust and disintegration."

Mr. Hay nodded. "We shall see to securing replacements." He turned to Isabel. "Would you like to stop for an inspection tomorrow on the way home from school? Perhaps there are some rooms you would like painted. I would suppose the kitchen and pantry ought to be whitewashed."

Isa shook her head in astonishment. "I can make do, sir! Really. I do not need new carpets, and I can paint bit by bit, if I'd like, after I have moved in."

"Hush, child." The deep-set eyes twinkled. "Do you want to go and spoil all our fun now?"

So it was out of her hands, and she tried to accept their good services with grace. Tuesday afternoon they decided on paint for the various rooms that needed it. Wednesday, Mr. Hay drove straight from the school into the milliner's shop and insisted Isabel select fabrics for curtains to replace the tattered remnants which Bertha and her friends had torn down and burned. He was so obviously enjoying himself that she bit her tongue half a dozen times or more and let him go on. The blacksmith was called in to shoe the little palfrey and check the wheels on the trap Isabel would be using. It seemed the whole village was aware of the project and had some sort of hand in it. *The teacher from America moving out to the moor house. Plucky of her, taint it? . . . Foolhardy. She'll go mad with the loneliness, mark my words . . .*

Thursday evening, as Isabel was correcting papers at the small desk in her room, Mr. Hay knocked at the door.

"Sorry to disturb you, my dear, but I have been thinking. You are sorely in need of furnishings: chairs to sit upon, a bed, a bureau for your clothes, a table or desk at which you can work."

She turned her chair round to face him. "I have already thought of those things. Helen Hunter told me there is a secondhand store in York. I shall get Mr. Phillips' brother, Damien, to drive me over on Saturday. I have a little money, and I am certain I can find much of what I need there."

"You might." Mr. Hay rubbed his narrow, stubbled chin thoughtfully. "But how unsatisfactory compared to what I have in mind."

Isabel laughed despite herself. "You must stop spoiling me, you must!"

He said no more, but questioned her concerning some of her students before shuffling out of the room. *I wonder how much longer he will be able to make it out to that school every day, as he does now,* Isabel wondered, with a sudden pang. *Once he is forced to relinquish personal supervision, things will alter quickly . . . and so much will be lost!*

At the door, Mr. Hay turned in that slow, deliberate way of his and gazed upon her intently. "You remind me of someone who used to live in the manor house, long before Willie John's time."

"Someone you remember?"

"Oh, vaguely. I was only a young fellow then." He grinned, and all the lines of his face became gentle, almost boyish. "See you in the morning, my dear."

Friday afternoon. Thanks to the efforts of so many, there was a chance she might be able to actually move into the gatehouse before the weekend was over. They rattled over the cobblestones past what Isabel liked to call Brontë Square, with the churchyard to one side of the lane, the belfried schoolhouse with the vicar's house beside it to the other, and the parsonage standing at right angles to the road, facing the church. The other side of the square, which was really more of an oblong, was open to the beckoning stretch of moorlands that lay beyond.

"Now look here, will you. Young Phillips has made it up from London in record time. That's his chestnut mare tethered beside the good vicar's."

Isabel looked, and felt a quiver of elation run through her.

"Never known him in all these years to make it here before nightfall." He winked at Isabel out of the corner of one eye, enjoying himself.

She realized he was slowing their own trap, bringing it to a halt while he sat there, thinking; she could almost see the wheels of his mind turning. When he spoke, it was deliberately, thoughtfully, like a ruminating animal, taking his own good time.

"I do believe there would be enough light left—if you hurry a bit, mind you—for you and the young gentleman to make it out to the gatehouse and take a quick look around."

Isabel reached over and squeezed his hand before she could stop herself. And before either she or Peter Hay had alighted, Damien stepped out of the house; he must have seen their arrival. When the professor's suggestion was presented to him, he showed immediate and candid enthusiasm.

"Good. I shall wait here with your brother. It has been a long while since we two have enjoyed a good talk."

The general sense of geniality and anticipation disarmed Isabel, and she said to Damien, as he stepped into the carriage and drew up the reins, "I am most anxious to view the transformation of my new abode and can think of no companion I would rather have with me than you."

"Which proves at least one thing: that the possibilities around here are terribly slim." Damien spoke the words flippantly, to cover the embarrassment he sensed in her revelation. But then he leaned close and for a moment placed his hand over hers. Some of the pulsing warmth of the sinewy fingers—of the very essence of the man—seemed to pass into her. They continued up the dark, close lane in silence. Words were not necessary to the comradeship both felt and did not wish to spoil.

❧

Isa had not been inside the house for two days. Even the boxes of her personal belongings, which she had packed up, had been delivered by the local dairyman in his lorry. She thought she would wait until Damien Phillips saw the empty rooms before asking him to drive her to York on the following day. She suspected nothing; she had not the slightest idea.

When they pushed the door open, Isabel gave a little start and put her hand to her mouth. But as her gaze took in more and more of her surroundings, she felt only dismay. "Oh dear," she sighed. "Whatever possessed Mr. Hay? What shall I do now?"

"Why, enjoy yourself. You are not thinking of returning these gifts? Think what you would do to the heart of the giver."

"But these are his wife's belongings, Damien—her bed, her boudoir table, her night stand, complete with the little Waterford crystal lamp."

"Yes."

"Please do not pretend that you don't understand."

"I don't, not entirely."

"These are precious to him. He has never in his life been without them. Do you know what it must have cost him to move these things here—to leave her rooms empty, denuded? Why did he do it?"

Damien placed his hands on Isabel's arms and turned her to face him. "He cares for you, and it brought him pleasure to help you. He is indulging himself as much or more than he is indulging you."

"Do you really believe that?"

"I know it to be true. Besides, this is good for him. He has been too deeply entrenched in the past, and that isn't healthy for anyone."

"It has not seemed to really harm him. He has a sharp mind and a gentle, generous spirit."

"You do not need to defend him to me. I'm quite fond of the old man, actually."

"I'm glad. So am I, much more than I appeared to be the last time we two talked."

"Then we are agreed on a very essential matter." Isabel could feel Damien's reluctance as he withdrew his hold on her arms, and they walked through the rooms together. "This place is well designed and solidly constructed," Damien observed. "A bit dark due to the scarcity of windows and the abundance of beams and woodwork, which overwhelms the rooms a bit."

"I like it that way."

"Well, good then. Do you think you'll be happy here?"

"For some inexplicable reason, I do."

"Then tomorrow we shall unpack and provide the finishing touches. I'll help you move and rearrange things however you'd like."

After a bit, when they realized the light was fading, they thought they had best be going. Damien handed her into her seat. In the enclosing dusk it appeared that both the sky and the earth were closing in on them. Layers of darkness, in shades from ash to ebony, like the enfolding strata, pressed against their little cocoon.

"The moors in the gloamin'," Damien observed, glancing around. "Do you think it will spook you?"

"I believe that it ought to," Isabel replied thoughtfully. "But I feel both eager and contented. Does that make any sense to you?"

"If you say it, it makes sense." The banter was in his tone again, but accompanied by a note of affection. Isabel—against all good judgment and reason—was sure it was that.

The dry weather held. Isabel and Damien spent all day Saturday unpacking, arranging, lining kitchen drawers and cupboards, and buying food and essentials. Midday they paused, prepared a picnic lunch, and ate it out on the moors. For the first time, Isabel crossed the South Dean Beck over the narrow shale plank known as Brontë Bridge. She sat upon the audacious outcropping of rock known as Ponden Kirk where, in the clear light, she could see such a far-flung expanse of valleys, farmlands, and distant blue hills that it left her feeling light-headed, as though she had no more substance than an eagle carried on the wind's ragged currents, as effortlessly as a feather or a fallen leaf.

"One feels small here, overwhelmed by the forces of nature," she observed.

"Precisely. No wonder the Brontë sisters grew up melancholy and broodish."

"Yet, something within is fascinated, drawn to that wildness, even while it mocks and repels all frail human lives that pass over it."

Damien regarded her intently. "You puzzle me more than any woman I have ever known, Isabel. Perhaps you should be the writer."

"Oh, no."

"I am fit for nothing but technical, logical prose, devoid of all imagination. But there is something in you . . ."

She pushed him away from her literally, with the tips of her fingers. "Stop it. I haven't any such pretensions. Mr. Hay says no work on earth is more noble and far-reaching than that of a teacher, and I love what I do."

"Even here, amongst these dark, benighted people?"

She smiled at his words. She smiled at his presence, the lightness that surrounded his being, that drew her out of herself in a way she had never experienced before.

When shadows began to slant across the hills, they laid their work aside and hiked back to the village, where they ate a hearty meal at The Black Bull pub. Isabel tried to imagine Branwell Brontë drinking himself to death here, but there was little of that atmosphere about the place now.

Later, however, when Damien walked with her to Mr. Hay's house, he took the same route she had taken the day she was caught in the storm; through the narrow, alley-like street—more of a passage really—entirely sided and covered over with bricks of stone. A sense of depression, cold and palpable, settled upon her, much as if someone had thrown a heavy cloak over her head.

"I do not like this place," she said with a shudder.

"This place?"

"This street." She fought down an almost uncontrollable urge to cry. "Don't you feel something here? Some presence—some sorrow . . ."

Damien linked his arm through hers and drew her a little closer, glancing at her face with that same curious expression that was beginning to disconcert her. "No, my little one, I feel nothing at all."

They came out into the light and air of the wider thoroughfare, and Isabel attempted to laugh off her fears, lest he begin to think her too unstable to live by herself on the moors. "Meetings tomorrow," she mused aloud. "And at the end of the day, I shall sleep in my new home for the first time."

"On the Sabbath. That is fitting."

"Yes." She suddenly felt that it was. "A benediction of sorts."

It was early yet when he said goodnight to her, but she wished to share one more tea with Peter Hay. This time she listened to his talk with genuine interest and answered his questions with an almost benign indulgence.

"Shall we make this a custom?" the old man suggested. "Saturday afternoon tea each week?"

"No, I might get caught up in my work of a Saturday," she responded. "Let us make it for the Sabbath instead."

It was agreed upon. But Isabel could not help wondering, as she prepared to sleep on the day bed in Edith Hay's little sitting room, what her weekends, in truth, would be like. Was Damien Phillips to become a customary, dependable part of them? She must not hope for that. She tried to remember what he had said upon their first meeting—surely he did not come weekly to his brother's, especially once winter set in. She could not expect—she dared not expect!

Sleep was a long time in coming. Tomorrow she would leave the village behind and embark on a life of her own in every sense of the word now. Why did she feel only elation—like an eager, inexperienced young school girl? Why did she feel such a strong yearning for the unknown experiences that waited ahead?

❧ Chapter Nine ❧

SHE TOOK POSSESSION QUIETLY, AS was fitting, insisting on good-byes at the churchyard, even with Damien. They had all eaten dinner at the vicar's house; he was in possession of a most excellent cook. They had toasted her health and given her advice, both in jest and in earnest. Seymour Phillips had patted her on the head, and Peter Hay kissed her cheek in farewell. She had wanted Damien to kiss her, too. But how could that be—how could she expect such a relationship with him? They were friends; she must remember that; *friends*. How could a man as radiant and clever as Damien fall in love with a woman as plain and ordinary as she?

All her aunt's words came rushing back at her, as cold as the blustery moor wind. She had allowed herself to forget; life was so different here than in Boston. She did not believe people thought of her as either old or uninteresting. She was the American. Mr. Hays was fond of her. *You cannot expect men to admire you. You are not pretty enough. Your features are too coarse.* But surely Damien admired her; surely she had not entirely imagined such a look in his eyes!

Such memories and misgivings assailed her as she trudged up the rough heaths. She knew well what she looked like, but she would not call her features coarse. She was not a petite girl, but long-limbed, with wide shoulders and a head that was big enough to support the weight of her heavy brown hair, almost mahogany it was so dark. Her brow and eyes were dark, too, large eyes set deep; Lawrence had said that her soul burned out of them. She had a Grecian nose, long and prominent, but her lips were full and nicely shaped, she thought, and the whole picture was not unpleasant. *Bold*. Perhaps that was the word for her features. Perhaps she frightened men off. She did not know how to appear weak and silly, or to show interest in vain banalities; she never had. Perhaps men, by and large, were ill at ease around women who stood nearly as tall as they did and appeared to be nearly as confident.

She drew a long sigh and lifted her face to the wind that seemed to be building in strength. *Do not let such unimportant things spoil this day*, she told herself. *Do not make yourself unhappy for no real reason at all.*

She reached the gatehouse and noted with satisfaction the clean windows, the swept, uncluttered yard, the welcoming air of the place. She let herself in with the key Mr. Phillips had given her, and the spirit of the room reached out to her. *Edith Hay*, she thought. *Those belongings which were hers still reflect her.* She took a long look about her. Though scantily furnished, the room was comfortable, with both couch and easy chair, and a tall candlestick oil lamp to shed ample light for reading. A fair store of wood was stacked by the hearth, and there was a cooking stove in the kitchen, as well as a large working table, and Edith's small writing desk in her room.

She walked through to her bedroom. The soft quilt that covered the bed had been Edith's, but how sweet and cozy it made the room look. She had never felt such care in her life as she was experiencing here among strangers. How odd that seemed.

Her eyes were drawn by a package wrapped in brown paper that lay on the coverlet. She picked it up in her hands. Her name was written across the surface in bold, fine strokes. She untied the wrappings which fell away to reveal a thick volume smelling of leather and embossed in gold lettering. *The Compleat Poetical Works of John Donne* the title read. What a treasure! Isabel hugged it to her, then gingerly opened the cover and saw the inscription inside.

Welcome home, Isabel . . . from a friend and admirer, Damien Phillips.

A friend and admirer. The words reached out and touched her with their warm restorative power. She sat down at Edith's desk, drew out a sheet of paper, and wrote him a thank you note; the first act performed in her new home. Then, effused with a sense of well-being and magnanimity, she penned a letter to Aunt Gwendolyn, the first she had written since her arrival in Yorkshire. She wrote at length and she wrote kindly, while the wind rattled the newly-caulked windows and whined down the chimney, and night came on.

The storm broke all at once, the heavens opening like a sieve. Listening to the wind, Isabel could think only of the tormented wail of the banshee shivering down from the vale of the dead.

At first the fury and the noise that accompanied it frightened her. She stood at the window hugging her arms to her body, acutely aware of her aloneness. *Is all this wrath and turmoil directed against me?* she wondered. *The stranger who has no right of place here?*

She turned away from the bleak aspect and lit the candles that stood in sconces along the far wall. Then she turned up the flame on the large kerosene lamp. But even that golden glow was not sufficient to dispel all the shadows that whispered along the floorboards and ceiling. *Is this some sort of a test?* she thought, pacing the room, whose quiet seemed eerie compared to the terrible sounds of the storm. So many dark images played through her mind, gleaned from books, fanned into greater life by her own imagination. *Are the moors trying to frighten me? to force me away?*

She forced herself to sit still in Peter Hay's comfortable chair and open a book. She held it in her lap for long moments, trying to make her eyes focus and her frozen mind concentrate. The elements battered her small fortress unrelentingly. She sat still, listening, thinking . . . and as the thought formed in her mind—vague and uncertain at first—she felt the rightness of it, and an almost instantaneous relief.

The wild moorlands are welcoming me, she realized, *with a display of their power and magnificence. They mean to impress me, they mean to delight me.*

She was bemused by her own reasoning, and the unaccountable clarity of it. She felt the painful tenseness within her relax. *Welcome home,* Damien Phillips had written. A singular choice of wording. *I am not here by accident,* she reminded herself, *but of my own choice. I was drawn to this place, this very place, so I will not concern myself with anything that will cause me to doubt or fear.*

Thus relieved she was able to actually read a bit, prepare her materials for the next day's lessons, and make preparations for bed.

Nevertheless, when it came time to put the lights out, she left one small night candle burning, safe in its earthenware bowl. The storm was still blustering unchecked, and she could not quite face darkness both within and without.

Isabel put on a cheerful face for Mr. Hay the following morning, convincing him that the storm had not disturbed her at all. "It was the moor's way of welcoming me," she told him, and her outlook charmed his own concerns away—and she chose to tell him of none of her struggles or fears.

That was Monday morning. Tuesday morning she dissembled for a second time.

"Did you sleep well, my dear? No storm to disturb you on this night."

She assured Mr. Hay that she had. She chose not to mention the face she had seen at the window. Perhaps she had only imagined it after all. The hour had been late. She had bent too long over her literature books, scheming lessons and schedules, and had straightened up, kneading the back of her neck with a tired hand, when she realized that there was an image in the window glass directly opposite her. She felt the hairs on her arms and neck stand on end, and her blood began to pump madly. She could not take her eyes from the burning, colorless eyes that stared into hers.

Then suddenly a lever within her snapped, releasing all her pent-up terror and rage, and she flung herself at the window and pounded the glass with her trembling fists, screaming at the intruder—flinging her fear at him like a weapon. She saw the eyes blink, and then the face went out, like a light.

She remained at her post, stretched taut as a wire, crying out threats she knew no one was there to hear. After she ceased, after the letdown left her drained and spiritless, she walked the rooms—her insides still churning, her nerves on end—for any flicker of movement, any sound, any small thing to alarm her again. Nothing. She waited a few minutes and repeated the process. Nothing but silence and a blank sheet of darkness her eyes could not penetrate.

She began to get ready for bed. *I was tired*, she told herself as she dressed hastily in her nightclothes. *Perhaps I did only imagine; perhaps it was a shadow made simply of moonglow and trees—a trick of light and shading that my mind took for . . .*

She dared not let herself think about it. She climbed between the cold sheets, her muscles tight, her heart pounding still. And she left the night lamp burning again.

That was the second night. The third night passed without incident; the fourth night as well. And another week of teaching was nearly over.

She had told her students about her new dwelling, describing it for them, sharing some of the excitement with them. They were reticent still, but she continued each day, as though she did not notice their lack of response. And, bit by bit, she became aware of a change.

Friday afternoon, as classes were breaking up for the week's end, Rachel Hill asked, "What is it like where you come from?"

"Boston is a big city compared to here, and one of the oldest in America. It is built by the sea, and the sea, like the moors, has its own sights and smells. There is a large common in the center of the city with trees and green grass and a pond."

"You like it there?"

"I like it very much. I have never lived anywhere else, until now."

"Aren't you frightened out there alone on the moors?" Lizzie asked, and six pairs of eyes watched carefully for her response.

"Sometimes, late at night," Isabel answered truthfully. "It is terribly dark, and the house is still, and the darkness also has strange, uncanny sounds of its own."

"Do you have lots of pretty things?" Dorothy piped. Little Dorothy, quiet and wistful, daughter of the frosty headmaster.

"You must all come and see for yourselves sometime. Would you like that?"

Isabel could have sung out at this first modest breakthrough. She liked these girls already more than she wanted to admit to herself. To be able to relax with them, get into their minds and spirits! She could hardly wait.

When Mr. Hay's trap arrived at the gatehouse, he asked Isabel if she would like to come on into the village with him. "You are welcome anytime, my dear, you know, if the loneliness gets to you."

She was grateful for his offer and told him so.

"Is that young fellow coming this weekend?"

"I am not sure," she answered truthfully. "But if he doesn't, I still have plenty to do."

Peter Hay patted her hand and let her have her way, waiting until she turned her key in the lock before starting his horse up again.

"I shall see you on the Sabbath, if not sooner," Isabel called back. "For church and for dinner!"

He nodded, his eyes crinkling up with pleasure. She could hear the sound of his conveyance rattling over the hard-packed road long after the small trap with its lone passenger passed out of sight. Save that departing sound and herself, there was no other sign of life here, and the hours of a long night ahead. Isabel hummed to herself as she changed into her work dress and prepared a simple supper. *Perhaps I should have gone with him*, she thought. *Then I could find out for certain if Damien has come.* She ate slowly, but the clock moved even slower as the long autumn night set in.

Despite her protestations to Mr. Hay, Isabel finished her chores by late morning, and the remainder of the day stretched ahead. *Something must have kept Damien in London*, she thought, *something unexpected, or he would have told me beforehand, even in the note he left with my gift, that he would not be coming.* She knew what she was going to do, but she felt foolish doing it, like a curious schoolgirl in search of excitement, intent upon frightening herself.

The day was cold, but there was little wind and no rain threatening. Isabel walked out into the open day: *The whole wide moors are my doorstep,* she thought. The leaves on the tall ash tree that stood by her door had turned a dark purple, like the color of crushed grapes. Oak, ash, and thorn . . . the sacred trees of Great Britain since the beginnings of time . . . She covered the half mile from her door to the manor house in no time and let herself in, wondering if she should call out in warning or greeting, lest Willie was there.

"Willie John . . . Willie John . . ." Her voice echoed in the cavernous space and bounced back at her. "It is Miss Emerson from the gatehouse . . . hallo—Willie . . ."

Nothing. The echoes receded into silence. Isabel walked through the mammoth front parlor with its heavy furniture and dusty paintings in ornate frames lining the walls. *Every English great house and castle has its requisite row of dead ancestors and ancestresses . . .* She gazed up at these with little interest, tracing her way to where the parlor opened onto a library of grand proportions. She gazed about her in astonishment. There were still hundreds and hundreds of books filling shelves that reached three-quarters of the way to the ceiling. *What a shame that no one touches them or reads them.*

Isabel reached out a finger and ran it along the spine of a thick leather volume that rested eye level across from her. Macaulay's *History of the Roman Empire*. Her fingers itched to draw it out and open it. *I wonder if Damien has ever seen this place? Next weekend I shall bring him here.* She walked from section to section, pausing when a particular title caught her eye. It would take more than a lifetime to read the books that were gathered and left idle in this one place.

Isabel rubbed her eyes and sat in one of the leather upholstered library chairs, aware of the dust that filtered out of the pores with a sigh as it accepted her weight. *What were the people like who lived here?* she wondered. *What was the man like who collected this library? Did he read his own books? Was there ever laughter in this room or the kind of searching conversation that heats up the mind?*

Looking about she realized that there were several display cases placed about the room in which stuffed fowl and small animals were displayed. She went closer to see: squirrels, moor hens, red foxes, weasels, martens, and an impressive variety of small birds from wrens, robins, finches, starlings, and hummingbirds to puffins, great horned owls, hawks, buzzards, and eagles—and a magnificent raven, his glossy feathers glistening purple here and there along the ebony stretch of his wings.

Isabel thought at once of the poem she was planning to teach to her young charges this coming week: "*Once upon a midnight dreary, while I pondered, weak and weary, Over many a quaint and curious volume of forgotten lore . . .*" She reached out the tip of a finger and stroked the satiny feathers. "*While I nodded, nearly napping, suddenly there came a tapping, as of some one gently rapping, rapping at my chamber door.*"

Without any thought at all, Isabel reached in and drew the handsome bird out. Stiff on his perch he lowered above her, an obvious bird of prey, his sightless glass eyes burning into her. *I must have him*, she determined. *I will merely borrow him to make this magnificent verse come alive for my students.*

She turned round, almost as though expecting to find someone to beg leave of. But, of course, the room was empty, with no sound or movement beyond. A thought came and she acted upon it, pulling out the long drawers of the big desk that sat in the corner until she found paper and pen. Ink—that was harder to locate. But at length she penned a note to the owner—*Willie John with his halt mind and his halt speech could not own a room like this, whatever powers might bequeath it him!*—and propped the paper in the empty space where the raven had been. Then she moved carefully back with her treasure through the library, the sitting room, the entry, finally out the door, much like a guilty and hopeful escapee.

"You will not object to a little adventure, will you, my pretty?" She spoke to the black bird aloud as she walked down the leaf-coated path to the cottage that hunched beneath its tufted thatch cap like a long, lazy elf.

It was a little indiscretion to borrow without permission, nothing more. She would return the raven unharmed in a day or two, and probably no one would be the wiser for her little incursion into a world of substance and beauty that had been left, quite ignobly, to die by itself. The presence of the bird, wild and enigmatic even in death, made Isabel feel strangely content and alive.

❧ Chapter Ten ❧

SATURDAY EVENING PETER HAY SENT A boy from the hostelry
with the dappled palfrey and small covered trap he had promised.
The next morning, Isabel drove to church both in comfort and style.

It warmed her heart when folks she scarcely knew paused to
greet her, or even to offer a smile. Some of these, she knew, had
worked on the cleaning and restoration of the cottage, and it distressed her not to be able to thank them, to acknowledge their many
kindnesses. She took her accustomed place in Mr. Hay's narrow pew
and remembered suddenly, with startling vividness, the pew in the
old Boston church where she had sat, squirming and miserable, while
pity and derision poured down upon her head like icy water. Here
she had found kindness and a degree of acceptance she had never
hoped for.

When the service had ended, Seymour Phillips shook her hand
warmly as she made her way out with the other parishioners. "Something must have come up," he said, lowering his voice and leaning
his tall frame toward her, "or I do believe Damien would have made
it up here."

Isabel smiled, touched by his kindly manner. *It is good of you to be
concerned about me*, she wanted to say.

Once outdoors she found herself looking about in hopes of
catching a glimpse of Willie John, who often hung around the outside of the church, but would never go in. She had not seen him
since she had taken up residence in the cottage. Had her presence
there scared him away? Might he be angry—look upon her as a
usurper? No, he did not appear to be capable of that sort of thing.

But later, at dinner with Mr. Hay, because the question had come to her, she asked, "Has Mr. Phillips told Willie John that I have rented his cottage? Indeed, was his permission required?"

"Noooo." Mr. Hay sat back in his chair, his eyes reflective. "Willie John is always strictly informed of anything that happens in regard to his properties, but I do not believe he retains much." His tone was doleful. "A monthly allowance is sent from the bank in York to Seymour, who passes the money on to Willie. He carries it about on his person, seldom using a portion of it, Isabel. His needs are modest, pathetically modest."

"Cannot something be done about that? Cannot someone educate him—make him understand?"

"Various people have tried, from time to time. He is not . . . receptive."

"He enjoys the way he is living?"

Peter Hay shrugged and wrapped his long arms round his body while Bertha warmed up his tea.

"Does he know—does he realize there are alternatives?"

"We cannot get inside his head, Isabel—you understand what I mean by that."

"Have you ever tried to get him into your school, give him some sort of training?"

"Yes, yes I have done so from time to time."

"From time to time, when someone is bothered by a few pangs of guilt, seeing him slink around the barns or back entries of inns, befuddled and hungry!"

Peter Hay smiled, but the expression was more of a grimace. "You have not been here long enough to judge, my dear," he said gently. "Best leave well enough alone where Willie John is concerned."

"And what of that beautiful house and all the land? Whose hands will it pass to when he gives up the ghost, or simply wanders off into the moors one day?"

"You shall have to ask your question of the vicar; I know nothing of that."

Isabel let the subject drop and enjoyed a pleasant evening with her old friend, leaving before the long shadows merged into a palpable darkness. She had a dread of being alone on the moors at night.

It took longer than it ought to have for her to unharness the palfrey, rub her down, and feed her, but she knew with practice she would become more adept. She fell asleep to the sound of the wind rustling through the dry leaves of the ash tree; a thin, raspy sound that made her think of insects in the tall grasses of the Common on warm summer nights.

Tuesday Isabel brought the raven to school, with an old piece of sacking to cover him, and secluded him in the little cupboard to which she had a key. The day fit itself to her purpose perfectly, the sky churning out darkness as thick as a witch's cauldron. When it came time for her afternoon poetry class, she lit a tall candle in the dim room and unveiled the black bird, his pinioned wings stretched out wide.

She sat the girls on low stools in a half circle round her as she half-read, half-recited the lurid tale. She gazed into their tense, upturned faces and drew upon all her powers of expression to make the rhythmical words, cadenced like an ancient forest chant, come to life in their minds.

> *Open here I flung the shutter, when, with many*
> *a flirt and flutter,*
> *In there stepped a stately raven of the saintly days*
> *of yore;*
> *Not the least obeisance made he; not an minute stopped*
> *or stayed he;*
> *But, with mien of lord or lady, perched above my*
> *chamber door—*
> *Perched upon a bust of Pallas just above my chamber*
> *door—*
> *Perched, and sat, and nothing more.*

The poem was long, but the girls scarcely moved or breathed. When they reached the stanza where the demented speaker cries: *"Tell this soul with sorrow laden if, within that distant Aidenn, It shall clasp a sainted maiden whom the angels name Lenore—"* Isabel realized that little round-eyed Dorothy had tears in her eyes.

And the raven, never flitting, still is sitting, still is sitting
On the pallid bust of Pallas just above my chamber door;
And his eyes have all the seeming of a demon's that is dreaming,
And the lamp-light o'er him streaming throws his shadow
    on the floor;
And my soul from out that shadow that lies floating on the floor
    Shall be lifted—nevermore!

Upon that last word a shudder passed through the listeners. After a few moments, Isabel shut the book and opened her hands in a gesture of invitation.

"We know about darkness," Rachel Hill said, "and things that are possessed or demented."

"You have many such stories and legends, I know. I should like to hear them," Isabel replied.

"The man was so unhappy," Lorna said. "I don't know anyone who is that unhappy."

"My mother told me that the young wife at the great house— Willie John's mother—was unhappy because she had a harsh husband who used her cruelly." Lizzie said the words matter-of-factly, and the comments continued, no one taking issue with what had been stated. *Part of local legend—or a simple statement of truth?* Isabel wondered; she found herself sincerely wanting to know.

Wednesday evening Isabel went to bed early. Perhaps if she had still been up and working at her desk, she would not have noticed the patter of stones against her window, or the sound would not have seemed so ominous. At first she put the sound down to the wind or the usual night noises. A sharp thud or two against the pane of glass, followed by silence; then the process repeated again. At length she arose and wrapped her night robe about her, but she was still loath to open the shutter and look out through the glass.

When at last she did, she saw a long white shape that seemed to be floating in the branches of the ash tree . . . and there was a sound that could not be the wind. Isabel put her hand to her throat and drew back from the window, her insides trembling with that weak, sick feeling that fear creates.

She stood stiff with attention, every sense of her body listening. There came a loud cry—what seemed like the shuffle of feet—and voices, muffled, yet somehow emitting confusion and fear. She hazarded a second peek through the window and saw three figures running in the direction of the village. They disappeared round the sharp corner that led to her cottage and the Rucastle properties. Before she could sort it out in her head, another figure stepped out from behind the ash tree. He was tall, but stocky of build, and his hair was like stiff hay, sticking out in all directions, like the false hair placed on a scarecrow. A *scarecrow* . . .

Isabel hurried to the door, undid the locks, and flung it open. "Willie John!" she cried into the wind.

The figure turned and bent nearly double, as though someone had struck him, and began moving away from her—slinking away from her into the darkness.

"Willie John, please! Please come and tell me what happened— I'm frightened."

She stood in the open doorway and waited, as the awkward figure slowly turned. He came shuffling back toward her, and when he drew close enough that they could make out one another's features, she smiled. "Please come in." She stood back from the door, encouraging him to enter, but he still gave her as wide a berth as he could.

"Who were those figures I saw running from here? Did you chase them away, Willie John?"

"Boys they were, from the village. Thought it would be great sport to frighten the school mistress." There was a strain of resentment in his voice that surprised her.

"You turned the tables on them, didn't you?"

Willie's thick lips parted and he grinned from ear to ear. "Serves 'em right! I don't like bullies; I've never liked bullies." He hunched his shoulders and rubbed his long arms with his hands, as though feeling or remembering some pain.

"Have some tea before you leave, Willie John." Isabel walked through to the kitchen and lit the flame beneath the kettle while her visitor took a long look around.

"You got this place fixed up nice, miss." His eyes had gone warm and unguarded. "You be as clever as Mr. Hay says you are."

Then Willie John had asked about her.

His eyes darted from place to place. When Isabel set his tea before him, he slurped it unconcernedly, ignorant of the fact that he may be lacking in good manners or even offensive. When he caught sight of the mounted raven where Isabel had placed it atop the mantelpiece in the parlor, he left his seat and walked over to peer at it closely.

"He be a nice bird, no matter what folk say," he crooned. *"Quoth the raven, 'Nevermore'* . . . *Quoth the raven . . ."* He savored the words on his tongue, enjoying the feel as well as the sound of them.

Isabel had come up behind him. "Do you know any more of the poem, Willie John?"

"I only remember little bits of what you read to the girls, with the bird sitting there big as life." He reached out his hand, stubby fingers awkward as a paw, and stroked the dusky feathers.

Isabel drew her breath in. "You heard me—you were there? Why didn't you come inside?"

He shrugged his shoulders again, such resignation in the gesture. "I don't b'long in a school. Too old. Can't learn, anyway."

Ignoring him, Isabel began again. "What other parts of the poem do you remember?"

It took him a few moments, but then he began, rather hesitantly, *" 'And the raven, never flitting, still is sitting, still is sitting . . .' "* He paused, chewing at a short fingernail, then picked up the strain again: *" '. . . his eyes have the seeming of a demon's that is dreaming . . .'* I like that part."

He was nearly word perfect; it was astounding. "Any more? The end. How does it go?"

And the lamp-light o'er him streaming throws his shadow
   on the floor;
And my soul from out that shadow that lies floating on the floor
Shall be lifted—nevermore!

Willie John spoke the words with a fervid satisfaction that was almost painful to watch.

"You have a sharp memory," Isabel praised. "Would you like me to loan you a copy of the poem to read for yourself?"

Willie hung his head; his shoulders slumped horribly.

"Wouldn't you like that?"

"Can't read, ma'am."

"Nobody every taught you?" Incensed, Isabel forgot to temper her response, and the big head sunk deeper. She moved close to him. "Let me teach you."

"I be too old for school learnin'."

"No, you aren't. Learning comes easier when you are grown, not harder." She had no idea whether that statement was false or true, but something impelled her to say it. "I would like to teach you, Willie John."

"You would?"

"Yes. It shall be our little secret, no one need know about it. Would that be all right?"

"You think I could learn?"

"You can learn, I promise you."

He backed away a bit, afraid of her zeal, afraid of commitment.

"Why don't you come tomorrow evening—just for a little while, and we'll see how you like it."

He nodded slowly. "All right, I can do that. All right."

She walked to the door with him. "Thank you for watching out for me, Willie John," she said, extending her hand. He squinted his eyes and hunched his shoulders, but at length touched her fingers briefly with his before slouching out of the room and lumbering into the night—moving like the moors themselves, in rough, ungainly undulations. The darkness soon snuffed out the sight of him. Isabel locked the door behind her and gathered up the tea things, her mind mulling over the events of the evening, testing a dozen different ideas and possible plans.

✌ *Chapter Eleven* ✌

Isabel spoke with Peter Hay the following morning about another matter that had come to her mind.

"Why does Willie John not own a horse of his own?"

"Because he's never expressed the desire or need."

"Mr. Hay! Expressed to whom? Do you men fancy yourselves the poor wretch's keepers?"

Mr. Hay placed his hand over Isabel's reassuringly. "He needs looking after, he always has, my dear."

"Can he care for a beast, does he know how?"

"I believe he does. He works now and again for the blacksmith, and for the various innkeepers, who set him to just such tasks."

"Then speak with the vicar about procuring a good horse for Willie. He can keep it in my barn with your sweet little gray—I call her Pilgrim, by the way. Has she another name?"

Mr. Hay's smile twinkled in his eyes, reducing them to slits, and twitched along the lines of his face. "Pilgrim will do."

"I'm glad. Where was I? Oh yes, Willie can board his horse with Pilgrim, and take care of both animals by way of payment."

Mr. Hay nodded slowly. "I believe that might do."

"Good. It would be a help to me, you know. I'm not much of a hand when it comes to such work; and once winter sets in . . ."

"Yes, your plan might work nicely."

They pulled up in front of the school. Isabel wished she could confide her other plan to Mr. Hay, but she had given her word to Willie. She took his arm and climbed down from the buggy. *Perhaps it will be just as well to surprise him and everyone else,* she thought. *That would be worth the waiting and the work, I believe.*

She said nothing to her students of the rude jest of the night before and wondered if she was only imagining the curious interest in some of their faces. Two or three had brothers of an age to be prime suspects. Perhaps Willie John would name the culprits for her if she asked him, but she was not at all certain that she wanted to know.

Tomorrow was Friday. Another week's end. Somehow the days had passed quickly, though she had not expected them to. Perhaps if Damien came he could help speed things up a bit. He seemed to be skillful at that.

Isabel ate early and had books and papers in readiness. She had not set a time, and as the clock reached seven and passed it, she began to wonder. But Willie John came. He was so scruffy—his coat unbrushed, his boots muddy, his hat weather-stained. *What would he look like scrubbed and dressed decently?* she wondered. But she knew she could not tackle everything at once and overwhelm him.

"I've a bit of stew left on the stove," she said, "and new bread that Bertha sent to school with Mr. Hay. Let me serve some up for you."

She moved before he could gainsay her, and while he ate noisily, she showed him the books she intended to begin with: McGuffey's Readers she had brought with her from Boston. He liked the look and feel of them, she could tell. He wiped his stained hand along his pant leg before lifting one of the red leather volumes and staring at the pages with reverence.

"Pretty pictures," he muttered.

"Yes," Isabel agreed, "and nice stories to go along with them. You soon shall see."

She started with the first primer, the very basics according to the phonics method: six letters in lesson one, two new letters and the *th* sound in lesson two. Willie sat tense and nervous for the first ten minutes, but once he had a pencil and a piece of paper upon which to practice, he forgot to be self-conscious and took to concentrating with a determination that shut all other sensations out.

An hour passed quickly, then another thirty minutes, and the clock chimed nine. With reluctance, Isabel closed the books and announced that tonight's lesson was done. Willie John rose at once, pulling his hat down over his ears, stammering out his thanks.

"You did well, Willie John. You did very well. The next lesson will be even better than this."

"When shall I come, miss?"

Isabel thought for a moment. *What if Damien comes up early, as he did two weeks ago?* "We shall have to wait until Monday, after the weekend." *Does he understand me?* "But then you shall have a lesson every single night, if you'd like."

That seemed to please him. At the door he turned back and grinned at her, in that way which had at first unnerved her so entirely and still disconcerted her. "You be like them," he said, "the other young ladies."

"What do you mean, Willie?"

"Emily and Anne and Charlotte. They wrote pretty things, didn't they? They read their books out on the moors. I see them there."

"Not really."

Willie John nodded vigorously. "Many a day I do, miss. Mistress Emily writes poems, and sometimes she reads them out loud; she don't seem to mind if I hear." In a singsong tone, without hesitation, he recited:

> What matters it that all around
> Danger, and guilt, and darkness lie,
> If but within our bosom's bound
> We hold a bright, untroubled sky,
> Warm with ten thousand mingled rays
> Of suns that know no winter days?

Isabel nodded, and he continued the stanzas until the poem was through. She drew his cold thick hands into her own. "That was—wonderful, Willie. A delight. Thank you for reciting it to me. Someday you shall write those words if you'd like to, and sooner than you think."

She said goodbye and let him go; his strange, ungainly gait marking him as surely as his slowness of speech. *Someone taught him those poems!* she thought, hugging her arms to her body, less against the cold night than the uncanny performance she had just witnessed. *Such knowledge does not come out of nowhere. But when did he learn them—and from whom? Who was the teacher, the one person in all of his life who has taken pains with him?*

She turned back to the silent room and the lessons she must correct and have ready for her students tomorrow, her unanswered questions still teasing and troubling her thoughts.

Friday was hers. She had thought of riding into Haworth with Peter Hay, but did not wish to appear too eager. If Damien Phillips came and desired her company, he knew where she could be found. There was no sign of Willie John, nor any other life in the wilderness around her, so she thought she would walk up to the manor house and return the raven to his rightful place in the library, before she became too accustomed to his presence on her mantel.

There was the taste of rain in the air, and the wide sky above her seemed to sag with its burden of clouds as she scurried up the path and into the gray, empty cavern that had once been somebody's home. She did not call out for Willie or anyone else, but went directly to the library, opened the cabinet, smoothed the black bird's feathers once more, and placed him where he belonged with the others. "I shall visit you again sometime," she said in a whisper. And she fancied the emptiness threw the echo of her own words back at her—or was that high, uneasy humming only the sound of the rising wind?

A chill trickled along her spine, and she closed the case hastily and glanced all around her, from side to side, as she began her way out of the room. The sound came again. This time it was more of a sigh . . . or a shudder. Isabel stopped, afraid to take one step further. Her exit was blocked by a presence . . . a shadow . . . no more than a gray-blue shadow at first. She did not want to see! She put her hand to her throat and attempted to close her eyes, but the black uncertainty of sightlessness, where imagination could grip her as well as the terrors of reality, was impossible to contemplate. She stood frozen, her eyes riveted of their own accord to the wavering, uncertain shape.

Though it neither moved nor grew in size or stature, the apparition seemed to embrace the whole room. Isabel tried to speak—or was it a cry that caught in her throat, sharp as a chicken bone, cutting her breath off?

As she looked, the vague shape took on form. She could see that it was a woman who stood facing her; a young slender woman with a thin, wistful face. The face was not the prettiest she had ever seen, but the sad eyes were gentle and very beautiful. The thin mouth turned down at the edges, not in an expression of bitterness, but poised it seemed, yes, poised on a point of melancholy that trembled across the space and touched Isabel with its cold, unrelenting pain.

She gasped. At the sound, the specter moved effortlessly closer, and as it approached, Isabel's fears began to dissipate and the choking sensation to relax. The woman gazed at her for a moment; concern—nay, pity—like a flame in her eyes. They stood thus a moment, gazing at one another, then the ghost woman began to fade, grow thin and insubstantial again, until she disappeared altogether, and there was nothing to look at but the long empty room.

Isabel walked from the library into the sitting room and sunk into one of the chairs there. She felt shaky and weak. She had never thought herself as the kind of person who would see a ghost. *Did the lady see me?* Isabel wondered. Because she had the distinct impression that the gaze of tenderness and sorrow had not been for her.

"Tea, m'lady? Shall I pour, or would you rather?"

Isabel jumped at the sound of the voice, and a delighted laughter answered her.

"I didn't mean to frighten you! But you look very much the part of the grand lady, sitting here in state, Isabel."

"I am glad you have come, Damien." She held her hand out to him. "I was just looking around a bit. Come, let's go outside again."

"I had a special assignment come along last weekend, one I was given no option of accepting or refusing. But I missed coming, missed seeing you." He took her arm and linked it casually through his. "Tell me all that's been happening, while I've been gone."

She told him many things, including the school lesson she taught with the raven. But she did not tell him of the face she had seen in the window, which she had fairly decided by now must have been Willie John. Nor did she tell him of the boys' cruel prank, nor the reading lessons with Willie; not yet, even for him.

"Will you dine with me this evening?" he asked, as they approached her cottage.

"I would be delighted," Isabel said.

"You have a beautiful smile, Isabel. What may I call you? Have you a pet name?"

She hesitated and Damien, watching her, waited. "Isa," she confessed finally.

"Is that what your friends back in Boston called you?"

"No. My whole life everyone has called me Isabel—except for my father—Isa was his name for me."

"I may use it?"

"Yes. I believe I would like that."

Damien took her hand and stroked it gently. "I'll hitch my chestnut to the trap, and we'll ride into the village in style, Isa."

Isabel smiled back and nodded, trembling to hear that name pronounced in his melodious voice.

❧ *Chapter Twelve* ❧

As THEY RATTLED OVER THE COBBLESTONED streets of the village, Isabel leaned back against the comfortable stuffed carriage bench and closed her eyes. *Should I tell him?* she asked herself for the hundredth time. *Would he believe me? What will his reaction be if I tell him about the lady in the library?*

Suddenly she lifted her head. "Why did you come this way?" she asked.

Damien turned to her. "What do you mean?"

"This road, this steep lane—why did you turn into it?"

"It's one of my favorite ways. I like how it is bricked all round, almost like a tunnel." He was watching her closely again. She could feel a sad trembling, like the sensation of weeping, pass over her and could give him nothing but a wan smile in response to his questioning expression.

"This place makes me feel sad for some reason—every time I have come here. Does that seem silly to you?"

"Silly? No. Not coming from you. No . . . there must be something . . ."

They came out into the light again and, with some effort, Isabel shook off the sensation.

"I am taking you to an inn on the Thornton Road," Damien informed her. "Something a little nicer than *The Black Bull* this time."

It was a nice inn, clean and brightly lit and ordinary, with a clientele who were largely strangers to them. Thus, Isabel was slightly surprised when a young man approached their table and stopped, gazing at both of them with an obvious curiosity. "Phillips, isn't it? Aren't you the vicar's brother?"

"Yes." Damien leaned forward amicably. "Damien Phillips. Just up from London for the weekend."

"Very good. Morris Whiting here."

"Of course! I remember you. It has been quite a number of years."

"Yes, I live in Keighly now, actually, and work over in York, so I'm not in the village much."

"Oh?"

"And who is your companion?" The stranger spoke with a nervous air, Isa thought, and his voice was thin, with very little timbre to it, and an obvious lack of feeling that made any expression seem forced and false.

"I'm so sorry." Damien glanced briefly at Isabel and, perhaps unconsciously, reached for her hand. "This is Miss Emerson, Isabel Emerson, from Boston, Massachusetts; Peter Hay's new teacher."

The red-haired man laughed deep in his throat, and his fingers, long and pasty in color, plucked at the ugly scarf that was tied there. "Yet another American transplant." He curled his lip in a look that could not be taken for anything but disdain, and the expression pinched his narrow features in a most uncomplimentary fashion.

"Well, we're quite happy to have her. She's really a gifted teacher."

Morris Whiting did not respond. He moved his eyes back and forth with an unease that was annoying.

"Good to see you, man." Damien bent over his food again. "Take care now."

With an ill grace the gentleman moved off. "That man is quite horrid," Isabel whispered. "Whoever is he?"

"Just one of the local chaps—a bit of a blaggard; big spender, fancy dresser, but I don't believe he has much to back him." Damien chewed a few bites of gravy-soaked beef before adding, "His mother was a raving beauty in her time, flaming red hair and bold, provocative features. But that was a long while ago. I believe she runs a boarding house in Bradford; dreadfully gone to seed now."

"You speak so coldly, Damien."

"Sorry, I didn't mean to."

"People like that . . . it's a sad thing, really."

"Yes, I suppose that it is." The careful, appraising look came into his clear blue eyes again. "I forget what kind of person I am with. I must disappoint you dreadfully, Isa."

"That is a strange thing to say."

"Not really. You are a bit extraordinary in your sensibilities and perceptions, young lady. Haven't I told you before?"

Warmed and relaxed, Isabel told Damien about her encounter in the great house. He was more astonished than she had thought he would be.

"I've never been quite sure if I believe in the reality of ghosts," he responded. "But now you've forced the issue a bit, haven't you? Singular that it should be you she appeared to."

"Yes. And yet, it wasn't quite like that. I felt more as though . . . as though I had intruded into her world and, if anything, she was unaware of me."

"Ah. That does make a difference. Well, the way you described her, I feel fairly certain your lady must be Willie John's mother."

"Willie John's mother was Rucastle's second wife, wasn't she? What do you know about her?"

"Basic facts, sketchy really, and most probably distorted by local legend."

"Tell me what you know, Damien."

"She was a frail little thing, always sickly, couldn't have healthy babies; nearly every one she bore died."

Isabel shuddered. "What about Willie John? Where does he fit in?"

"Firstborn. Had several daughters born dead, or who died shortly thereafter, then another son who lived. Of course, the old man was elated, because Willie had never been quite normal, you know, right from the start."

"If he is as dull as people think him, how does he know so much about the Brontës—facts and figures, even random quotations from their writings?"

"That is quite remarkable, isn't it?" Damien shrugged his shoulders. "The man's over forty years old, Isa, and he lives in a world of his own."

"He's been given no other choice! I don't believe he ever had a choice, Damien!"

"True. But the point is, who knows what goes on with a fellow like that?"

"There may be reserves there?"

"There must be something for him to retain what he does; much of it, I would suppose, from hearsay only."

Isabel was elated. "Do you remember the old man at all?" she asked.

"No, he died the year I was born. His normal son, the one he pinned all his hopes on, died as an infant. Then, it seems, he turned on both his wife and his eldest son. He used to roar out that they both lived just to mock him."

Isabel remembered the misery in the dead woman's eyes and felt pity, like a terrible ache, rise up in her.

"Sarah—that was her name—became very ill, and legend has it that he would not care for her nor allow a physician to see to her. It was whispered that she died a painful and lingering death."

Isabel put her hand up, as if to stop him.

"Why, Isa, you are pale as a ghost yourself! Would you like me to stop?"

"Yes, after you answer one more question."

"Anything, little one."

"Anything?"

"Heaven help me, yes; ask me anything, Isabel." The gentle bantering tone was in his voice; he did not know how it disarmed her.

"Would you help me do a kindness for Willie John, Damien? It is very important to me."

"Important to you. Why should that be?"

She demurred, wishing she could tell him more. "I suppose I've developed a sympathy for him."

"I thought he repulsed you."

"He did—in the beginning. Oh, never mind that, Damien. Will you help me or not?"

"I gave my word, didn't I? Yes, you tell me what it is that is churning in that incredible mind of yours, Isa, and I will do all I can to help."

"I am very fortunate to have you as a friend and advocate," Isabel answered, and her whole heart was in the words.

"It pleases me to have you think so," Damien answered.

Isabel told him her plan, and he thought it, in substance, a good idea. "I like the fact that Willie John might be there to help you. I believe he is relatively competent where such things are concerned. But he might make a royal nuisance of himself; you must be prepared for that eventuality."

"And ask myself, is it worth it? I believe that it is."

"Very well, then. We shall get a fine horse for Willie John. And you are right—we should have done this a long time ago!"

They drove back to Haworth slowly, in no hurry to end the intimacy of being alone together.

"Two days ahead of us," Damien mused. "And I must tell you now, most lamentably, that I shall not be able to be here next weekend, so we must make the most of these days."

Why does he speak to me in this manner? Isabel agonized. *Do I dare believe that he cares for me?*

"What brought you here, Isa?" Damien asked suddenly.

She turned large, uncertain eyes on him. "Fate brought me here," she answered, "though you may laugh at the notion." She proceeded to tell him of her broken engagement, of the stifling nature of life with Aunt Gwendolyn, of her need to discover—not only new things, but what was inside herself.

He listened with that earnestness which was so endearing. "And what of the future?"

The words were so softly spoken that she was not sure she had heard him aright. "One step at a time," she answered. "I dare look no further."

"Why do you dare look no further?" Damien asked.

Her heart was pounding. Where was he leading her? His questions seemed unkind, unfair. A mild resentment tugged at her heart.

"It is all I can do to handle the present." She tried to introduce a lightness into her tone, but she possessed no ready wit nor easy humor, as he did.

"I have never had much of a desire to marry," Damien said, and there was nothing humorous about his tone now. "I think I've been afraid; well, I know I have. If you do not love someone, you cannot lose them—cannot suffer."

Isabel could not help herself. She put her hand on his arm and stroked it, her spirit yearning to comfort him.

"I realize my position is a cowardly one," he continued, still unable to recapture the unassuming tone.

"No. Those who feel deeply suffer most. It is only human to shun those things that cause us great pain." *Is he trying to say that he is afraid to love me? afraid of my leaving him, hurting him?*

They lapsed into silence, but it was not a comfortable silence. The dark moors seemed to close in on them. Isabel moved closer to Damien and rested her head against his shoulder.

"Fear is a terrible thing," she said, "but loneliness is far more terrible. To live always alone, with no one to care for, no one to turn to . . ."

"Yes, that would be insupportable. That would be a mere travesty of life, hollow and meaningless."

His hand groped for hers, and when he found it, he held it tightly, as though somehow that grasp would have the power to unite them; transmit strength to strength, tenderness to tenderness, shutting out the ever-present dangers and uncertainties that lurked just out of sight.

❧ Chapter Thirteen ❧

THE VICAR HAD HIS DOUBTS, BUT HE allowed his younger brother and the American schoolmistress to talk him into it. Monday morning, bright and early, he went to market and selected a dependable animal that would suit Willie John's purposes. But when they presented it to him, they could not get it through his head that the horse was really his.

"Mine to ride whenever I like—asking mistress's leave here?"

"No, Willie. Yours entirely," the vicar persisted. "It is your money that purchased him, and you may do with him as you like."

"Not my money, his! And he did not want me to have it, did he?" Willie scratched at his ear with a dirty finger. It was an annoying habit, like all of his habits. But Isabel thought of the tender expression on the pale lady's face, and a sense of sadness welled up in her.

The vicar persisted until he at least felt certain that Willie John understood he was to care for his mount and the teacher's. And, unaccountably, this seemed to please him.

"Well, get acquainted with your beastie, figure out what you'd like to call him, Willie," the vicar suggested, as he walked out of the barn with Isabel. "I hope you will not regret this," he said to her, a bit gloomily. "It doesn't take much for Willie to make a nuisance of himself."

"Thank you for the warning, but I'll be careful," she assured him. She stood and waved her hand as he drove off toward Haworth and was soon hidden from view by the sharp curve in the road that further isolated this lonely place. *I have my work cut out for me,* she thought. But she had no regrets, at least not yet, about taking it on.

October was drawing to its end. Even through two long weeks of not seeing Damien, the days seemed to go by too fast. Isabel was teaching her girls what she called "representative literature," a sampling of French, Italian, German, Scandinavian, and Russian literature, with sections to come in English—and American, of course. She was through the primers and into the second reader with Willie John. He was like a dry sponge. *Bereft*. That was the word that came to Isabel's mind. Bereft of so much.

Isabel found herself missing Boston: the abundance of beauty that autumn showered with such profusion there; the wooded hills; the piles of fragrant squash and pumpkins; the Common blazing with a riot of color; the flavor of Indian summer on the sea air, languid, smoke-tinged, mellow. *Has my letter reached Aunt Gwendolyn?* she wondered. She walked the drab, unobstructed moors, and Boston seemed a world away, inaccessible. *Will Aunt Gwen even answer me? And if she does, will it be all advice and scolding?* She could not imagine the two of them corresponding, sharing impressions and experiences with the open enthusiasm of trusted and trusting friends.

Everything back home was so ordered, so predictable. Her life in Yorkshire had none of that. Even closing her eyes, she could not bring up Lawrence's features; he was as hazy as a faded photograph. Was he married by now? She could not remember when the date had been set for. *What if I had married him?* she conjectured curiously. *What would I be doing right now? Would it have altered me? not only for the present, but for always; not only the outward patterns of my life, but what I am inside myself?* It would have to have been, for the moors had already altered her, reformed her way of seeing things, even of feeling things. And she marveled at how this was so.

On All-Hallows Eve, there was a party at the school with games and jack-o-lanterns, mulled cider and warm apple pies, made lovingly by a dozen different mothers. The girls were ecstatic, because the young men of the several villages had been invited. Isabel watched the youthful figures dancing, their graceful movements echoed in shadow against the high walls. She felt very old, very removed from their world of frivolity and naïveté. How brief, how often wasted, that magic time was before the harsh realities of life began to make themselves known, and the most innocent heart was forced to put away its frail childish garb, woven of hopes and dreams, for the heavy cloak of responsibility. It had ever been so. Her heart ached for them, as it did for the girl who had once been herself.

The teachers were there in official capacity as chaperones, and those who were married had partners to dance with, but no one asked her to dance. Headmaster Hopkins was on no more than polite speaking terms with her; he refused to progress farther than that. Arthur Thomas, Frank Martin, and Paul Kennedy had grown accustomed to her, but they would not cross barriers, would not risk destroying the careful fabric of their superiority to the American, the outsider. Strange how the people of the village accepted her with very few questions asked; but then, she did not threaten them. They were secure in their age-old roles, just as her male colleagues desired to be. Violet Massey and Helen Hunter were another matter. As women in common, they had relaxed their guard against her. She could talk to them of everyday things, and for a time, at least, forget the differences between them.

"Could I ever really belong here?" she asked Helen one day, her thoughts upon Damien.

Helen blinked in honest surprise at the question. "I say, if a person feels like she belongs, then she does. You could live in one place for fifty years and still be an outsider. It's all in here." She put her hand on her heart. "You know what I mean."

Isabel did know. And she wondered if she had ever, really, belonged anywhere; or if her heart would always stand awkward, unsure, and apart?

Guy Fawkes Day on November 5th was a bigger holiday in England than Halloween. Damien came up for the celebration and helped light the huge bonfire in the center of town. There was drinking, reveling, and a tension in the air that made Isabel feel as though a thunderstorm was building, building—about to break over their heads.

People dressed up and marched in processions, singing lustily, if somewhat incoherently. Damien knew, watching her expressions, that the revels were not only overwhelming, but distasteful to her.

"You ought to consider becoming a vicar's wife, Isa," he teased her. "Evelyn never came out on this night. She said she felt the powers of darkness unleashed around her."

"What of your brother?"

"He comes to keep watch on the rest of them, for what good that might do!"

"I agree with Evelyn," Isabel admitted, "and it is a rueful day, you know, when women's wisdom is ignored."

"There you go again!" Damien regarded her thoughtfully. "We'll go inside as soon as we dance round the bonfire. You have to do that."

She did not want to. She nearly persuaded him otherwise. And if she had, the freakish, macabre little tragedy would have played itself out.

The fire was huge, the roar of it more fearsome than the wind's roar. The dark shapes ringing it, their faces half-mottled in shadow, appeared otherworldly and ghoulish. Isabel tugged at Damien's hand and shrank back.

When a bevy of rough-faced, rough-clothed men danced up, staggering beneath the weight of a man-sized scarecrow, Isabel forgot herself and cried out.

"It's only an effigy, stuffed with straw."

"Are they going to burn it?" She averted her face from the spectacle. The lolling head looked too real, the limp arms, stretched out and helpless!

The burden shifted and slid in the men's clasp, and they tossed it amiss—rather than landing atop the pile, in the heart of the flame, it slid down the stack of smoldering branches and bracken. One of the feet, with its worn, hob-nailed boot, nearly grazed Isa's leg.

She stared aghast at it. Then comprehension bit at her, and she came instantly to life—calling out to Damien, but not waiting—tugging at the thick leg herself. Those around her moved back a bit, watching the crazed woman with interest; but such sights were not uncommon on Guy Fawkes night.

"Help me, Damien! Help me!" She did not realize that the tender skin on her hands was scorched, that a crumbling fagot burst into golden spray and sent stinging red cinders against her arms.

Only when they had dragged the body a safe distance away did she straighten out, spent and breathing raggedly. Damien put his arm round her shoulder and attempted to draw her close. "It's but a scarecrow—dressed like a man and stuffed with straw, Isabel!" He spoke as if to a child.

She gazed up at him, the red flames reflected in her eyes. "It is Willie John someone threw on the fire!" she said.

Then she was on her knees, bending over him—calling to him, shaking the slack shoulders, trying to lift the big head. Damien did not truly believe her until he got some of the fellows standing near to help him lift the body onto one of the hay wagons nearby. Then his own eyes, and those of his companions, confirmed her wild statement. Someone carrying a torch shined it into his face. "Is he hurt?"

"He be drunk," came another voice.

"Do you think that he's dead?"

At Isabel's insistence, they carried him into the vicar's lighted kitchen and laid him on the long slab of a table, and they determined that he was breathing.

"He's dead drunk."

"He's been knocked out cold. Look at the great purple bump on his head."

At the vicar's observation, the rest of the group grew silent, and the housekeeper came forward from down cellar and shooed them all out of the house. Damien was working the muscles of his jaw, and his whole face looked tense and tight.

"Do you believe it was an accident?" he muttered under his breath. But nobody answered him. At length the vicar spoke, just as softly, "It could have been a nasty prank."

Isabel thought of the boys outside by her ash tree. "Intended to end this way?" she asked.

Seymour Phillips ran his fingers through his thinning hair distractedly. "It is possible that in the excitement, someone mistook his body for that of the scarecrow. These fools are so befuddled with drink, half of them would not recognize their own mothers!"

The four people in the room looked at one another and Nancy, the housekeeper, clicked her tongue and began to prepare a hot poultice for the discolored bump.

"Is that all the explanation we're going to get, vicar?" Damien demanded a bit huffily.

"Probably so." Seymour's voice sounded drained and tired. "Most likely we'll discover no more of this business; not tonight, not ever!"

They moved Willie to the couch, and Isabel sat beside him, applying cool cloths to his forehead, until he came round. "Who would want to hurt Willie John?" she asked Damien, with wide, frightened eyes.

"Perhaps . . ."

"No. Someone intended to hurt him. I feel it. Though I cannot imagine who in the world, or why."

⁖⁞ *Chapter Fourteen* ⁖⁞

ISABEL WAS GLAD OF AN EVENING OUT. At times her seclusion seemed to press down on her and confine her whole world to that one lonely stretch of inhospitable earth and sun-starved sky. It was Tuesday evening, and Peter Hay had invited her home to share one of Bertha's fine dinners. She enjoyed both the food and the company and the almost comforting presence of a house that had both been lived in long and loved.

The slow realization came over her that here she was relaxed entirely; feet stretched out to the fire along with Peter, her hand wrapped round a warm mug of tea, Bertha's warm flannel cakes and Yorkshire scones waiting for a generous smearing of jam and a dollop of cream. *I was not aware of how tense I have been out at the cottage: always listening, always watching, always mindful of the solitude, like an alien presence.* It distressed her to realize this. *Yet, I love it there,* she reminded herself, by way of defense. *I am not unhappy.*

Bertha brought Mr. Hay a glass of water with which to take his nightly medicine, but when he reached for the bottle he realized that the pills were all gone.

"Meant to restock on Saturday," he lamented, "but it slipped my mind entirely."

"Let me go for you." Isabel rose and stretched. "I could use a bit of exercise, and I'm seldom in town."

She had wrapped a scarf around her neck, buttoned her coat against the rimy November air, and sallied forth before she realized that the chemist's shop was situated in the narrow, brick-arched lane she always recoiled from. She could not avoid it now. She walked resolutely, her shoes clattering against the moist, uneven stone pavement, and once or twice she felt herself slipping on a particularly worn, smooth spot.

She collected the tablets in no time and walked out into the darkness that had thickened during the brief moments she had been inside. The sky was coal black with only a thin gray line marking the horizon. Most of the shops were locked and dark; the two or three that yet had their lights burning appeared like faint beacons in the sea of night. But Isabel was walking away from them to where nothing but the aged stones, dripping and lichened, stretched before her; she wanted to cry.

She walked desolately on for a few yards, then sat down on a wide doorstep to retie one of her shoes. She realized that she was trembling, and her eyes were swimming with tears. This unaccountable reaction frightened her. *What is the matter with me?* she agonized, hugging her knees to her body and trying to summon up the resolve to go on.

"Miss Emerson, is it you? Whatever—have you been hurt, my dear?"

The vicar was down beside her in a moment, all solicitation. Isabel blushed, her mind fishing for some plausible explanation, but to her surprise the truth tumbled out.

"This place—this lane—has an uncanny effect upon me," she confessed. "I detest it, I dread it."

The eyes watching her were serious; there was no laughter or mockery in them. "Do you know why? Tell me more."

"There is no explanation! I feel an unaccountable sorrow every time I enter this enclosure. I feel this sorrow so deeply that I want to sob in despair, as if I have just lost my best friend."

Seymour Phillips rocked back on his heels, his expression thoughtful. "That is singular, most singular, especially since it happens to you."

"What do you mean?"

"Well, the nature of the place. There *is* an explanation as far as that is concerned."

Isabel still watched him expectantly, so he continued.

"Something terribly sad did happen here once, and sometimes those events leave impressions—the essence of the event never quite dissolves or dissipates. I do not entirely understand it myself, but there seem to be many such spots throughout Great Britain."

Isabel dabbed at her eyes. With an almost morbid expectancy she encouraged him, "What terrible thing happened here?"

"Tragic more than terrible. A young man of my acquaintance collapsed and died in this alley; indeed, only half a dozen feet from this spot."

Isabel's breath constricted, and the sadness washed over her like a cold, stunning wave. She gripped the arm the vicar extended.

"An excellent young man—happened twenty-odd years ago. I haven't given it a thought in a long while." He gazed into the darkness, remembering. "He was a stranger in these parts, but I grew most fond of him."

Isabel drew a deep breath. *Could it be this, the death of a stranger twenty years ago, that overwhelmed her?* "Why me? Why should I feel it?"

Seymour Phillips sighed. "I have no answer for such a question. There must be something within you that is in tune, that responds to elements not generally discerned by others . . ." He let his explanation trail off and helped her to her feet. "I'll walk the rest of the way with you."

"Thank you, I'd like that."

They moved quickly, and Isabel purposefully kept her eyes straight ahead.

"How is Willie John working out? Does he remember to come of an evening and feed the horses?"

Isabel thought of the night lessons that Willie never missed or was seldom late for. "He is quite dependable, really."

"Well, that is a welcome surprise."

"Have you thought any more upon what happened Guy Fawkes Night? Have you any idea . . ."

Seymour shook his head. "I have hinted around a great deal and pinned several young rascally fellows most uncomfortably with the force of my gaze. Did you not notice the sermon I preached that would have driven a good wedge of warning into the hearts of any of the guilty who may have been listening?"

"I remember."

"Well, that is the most I can do. I can go only so far into a man's conscience as he will allow me."

They reached Mr. Hay's house, and the vicar was prevailed upon to come in and finish off the rest of the flannel cakes. It grew so late that Isabel accepted the offer pressed upon her to stay the night. She had brought along night clothes and toiletry articles, just in case. But the day bed was too short and narrow, and she tossed and turned, aware of the sounds of the village, more than she remembered, magnified in comparison to the silence she was accustomed to. She laughed, a bit piqued at herself. Boston was a metropolis compared to this village, and she had been perfectly at ease there. It frightened her a bit to think that she could have changed so much.

Is there a bit of the recluse in me? she wondered. *If I lived here for years, would I come to crave and protect my solitude and desire the fraternity of my fellow humans less and less?*

She fell asleep wondering, vexing herself with questions that she knew did not need to be asked.

Folk talked so gloomily about the terrible winters in these parts that Isabel hastened to plan the little party she desired for her students before the dread season set in. It was to be a tea at the schoolmistress's house at eleven o'clock on a Saturday morning. Bertha offered to assist her with the baking of cakes and little goodies, and even Willie helped in the preparations by ranging far over the dried knolls and crags in search of some fair weeds with which to adorn the table. He returned bearing late bramble leaves, stiff and crimson; the pale golden rosebay willow stalks; and ochre-red dock wort; altogether a stunning array. Isabel arranged them in a wide-mouthed crock and placed them in the center of the table.

When the eight girls who were able to come had all arrived, they set out at once for a walk—to work out the fidgets and giggles. It was a brisk, windy day, but the exercise stirred up their blood and made them forget how cold their extremities were.

There was more to see in the dreary, color-washed landscape than Isabel had ever imagined. With Willie John as guide, they discovered a dozen different kinds of toadstools: the sulphur-tuft of rich orange and yellow, which grew beneath the debris of dead wood; the brilliant purple-gill, beneath a scraggly stand of pine trees; some that were shiny brown; some deep blue-black; some pale yellow or even pink. They saw many starlings, of course, and discovered a handsome green woodpecker on the trunk of a twisted old oak. A cheerful song thrush, soon joined by two of his mates, perched on the bare, leafless bough, singing as sweet as if it had been the first day of spring.

The girls relaxed, so that when they sat round the table, cold and hungry, and tea was poured, they forgot to be shy and chatted amongst themselves as though Miss Emerson was a trusted friend, not the sometimes austere school mistress.

"My sister is going to marry Morris Whiting," Lizzie Lindsay announced with an air of some importance.

"A wedding! How romantic!" Laura quipped. "Will she let you be one of her bridesmaids?"

Lizzie sniffed disdainfully. "She thinks I'm too young. Besides, I don't like Morris Whiting. I think he is a rude, self-centered boar."

Isabel had perked up at mention of that name.

"Why is she marrying him then?" Charlotte demanded.

"Because she believes he is very rich and very clever and that makes him a "desirable catch."

"Do you think he is rich and clever?" Dorothy asked hopefully, for she did not want to see the bright bubble burst.

"I already told you what I think." Lizzie shrugged her fine, slender shoulders. "It's her business—as she so often tells me. Besides . . ." She bent her head close to her best friend, Rachel Hill, and the others leaned forward, too.

" . . . Claire isn't the prettiest of girls, is she? Mother says I inherited all the looks," she smiled whimsically, "and Father says I inherited the brains."

"I like Claire, though," Dorothy defended, "she has always been nice to me."

"That's because you are not her little sister."

The girls giggled in agreement, and the conversation took another turn. But Isabel was left with the same cold feelings she had experienced in Morris Whiting's company. If Lizzie's sister, Claire, was indeed a nice girl, what a waste to think of her marrying a cold fish like Whiting. She smiled at her own unintended pun and went back to the serving. Goodness, Bertha had been right to bake as if for a dozen men rather than eight dainty young girls. Not one bun or scone or frosted cake remained when they pushed back their chairs and rose to take leave of their hostess.

"Thank you! Thank you ever so much for having us!" "It was awfully pleasant." "The sandwiches were smashing." "This is such a dear little place!" "I should like to set up housekeeping in a cottage just like this when I am grown." "Are you going to really set up housekeeping with the vicar's handsome young brother?"

This last came from Ruth, who did not say it to heckle, but out of the sheer romance of the idea. So Isabel colored a little and let the remark, and the eight sets of curious eyes that followed it, go.

In fact, when they did traipse out at last and pile into Mr. Kennedy's wagon for the ride back to Haworth, Isabel leaned against the doorframe, amazed at how exhausted she felt. They did not wear her out in this manner during school hours, thank goodness. But each girl, in her way, was a dear, and Isabel grew more and more fond of them and was happy to be able to provide a diversion from the ordinary routine of their lives.

Willie John had retired to the barn as soon as the walk was over, so she took him out a large mug of hot tea and a plate of treats she had secreted in a cupboard. He shuffled his feet and stuttered a bit, trying to thank her.

"It is I who am indebted to you! You made our day entrancing and helped me entertain those high-strung young ladies. Otherwise, what would I have done?"

He grinned, stuffed a biscuit into his mouth, and slurped his tea up to soften it. She had not yet taught him table manners and wished she could begin to do so right now. But she knew from experience that he would merely grow defensive and quiet, and she would lose more ground than she ever would gain.

She lingered a few moments to feed Pilgrim a bit of old apple and let her nuzzle her shoulder, then wandered back into the house to clean up and tidy a bit before treating herself to half an hour curled up on the sofa with Sir Walter Scott's *Marmion*. Her modest tea party had been a success and that pleased her immensely. Perhaps she would write and tell Aunt Gwen all about it. Why had Aunt Gwen not answered her yet?

Well, she would not let that thought spoil the little glow her day had left with her. She had succeeded; she had brought pleasure to others. Nothing should be allowed to spoil that.

❧ *Chapter Fifteen* ❧

THE FOG WAS THIN; "WITCH'S TATTERS" they called such a mist back home. It was early yet, a thick shepherd's pie was bubbling in the oven—enough for both herself and Willie John—and Isabel felt there would be time for her to slip up to the manor house. It would just take a moment. She knew right where the book was, having noted it on her last visit—a wonderful edition of Goethe's works which she felt she must have for her lessons the following day.

She threw on a cape and headed into the haze, whose cold particles clung like brittle bits of varnish in her hair. Once inside the house she hesitated, her gaze darting involuntarily from place to place. Would the ghost lady be waiting in some shadowy corner or behind one of the tall chests or sideboards scattered throughout the long rooms?

She reached the library with no incident and for a few moments was immersed in an entire shelf of German writers: Lessing, Kant, Schiller, Heine, and several with whom she was not familiar. What a treasure was here! She stroked the spines with her finger, wondering if she could make Willie John understand her desire to borrow and read these books. She could make a proper list of the ones she removed and the dates when she took them.

She stopped. It was not a sound she had heard, but a movement she had caught in the corner of her eye—off somewhere to her right. She whirled in that direction, her muscles tense, her heart pounding. She saw it again, more distinctly—and at the same time there came a vague sound from the opposite direction . . . someone was whistling, she was sure of it: a brave, almost martial tune, whose notes swirled and echoed through the empty rooms.

She heard more sounds from behind her, but she dared not move her eyes from the apparition that hovered indistinctly a little to the right of the fireplace. *I'll cry out!* she thought, but her mouth was dry, and she was afraid the sound of her voice might startle or anger the personage before her.

When at length she heard footsteps—real footsteps with weight and substance to them—and a human voice repeating the melody of the whistle, she hazarded one glance behind her to see Willie John approaching, crumpled hat stuck atop his untidy hair, his expression casual. He caught sight of her, and his dim eyes lit up.

"Willie!" Isabel hissed through clenched teeth. "Look ahead. Do you see her—the ghost, the lady—there to the right of the mantel?"

He nodded. "That's me mother, Miss Isabel. I sees her often when I come here."

She glanced again at the indistinct shape, whose definition was fading, leaving behind her the same sense of tender sorrow Isabel had felt the first time she saw her. "I'm sorry." She whispered the words aloud. "I am sorry about your son, Sarah. It must have been difficult to leave him like this, with no one to protect or understand him."

She felt the desolation lift as she spoke, and the air became light again, and there was no sign left of the essence to which she had addressed herself.

"She'll come back. She always does."

"You said you see her often?" Isabel remembered, turning her attention to Willie John.

"Well, not every time I come here. But lots of times. There 'ave been long years, miss, when she's been away."

"Yes. How old were you?"

"Eight years, no more. Then my father died the year after, but I was not sad to lose him."

"Not at all?"

Willie shook his huge, rough head emphatically. "He were a mean one, my father were. An' he had no love for me."

What could she say? "You were young and he frightened you, but that doesn't mean . . ."

"No, mistress, he told me, and many a time, too. Told me how worthless and disgusting I was. 'You should 'ave died, not all the other fine and normal ones. Why wasn't it you the Lord took, or the devil—whichever it was.'"

Willie's voice was emotionless, as though he were merely reporting a fact, or reading from a page in a book. But Isabel's insides twisted at the unsightly picture his words drew. "I'm sorry, Willie," she said. "It was shameful for him to speak to you in that manner."

"No matter, 'twere a long time past; and besides, it were true."

"No it wasn't—no it isn't! He made you believe . . ." Isabel hesitated. He was less than normal, she could not deny that and expect to maintain credence in his eyes. "You are so much more than he made you think, Willie John. Look at how quickly you are learning to read. You have a good mind. Your mother thought so, didn't she?"

A soft expression came over the ungainly features. "She did love me, I know that. She did tell me nice, happy things."

Isabel's smile trembled a bit. "I am glad you remember her, Willie John. I am glad you remember those times."

She took him to the wall of books and explained what she wanted to do, and again he seemed puzzled that she should be asking permission of him. "These books are yours," she repeated. "Do you not own Rucastle House and everything in it?"

Willie John shrugged his rounded shoulders and scratched at his cheek. "So they do tell me. But what does it mean, mistress? I cannot live here for want of money to heat and light the great rooms. I cannot work the land. I cannot read the books, or write letters."

"Someday you shall, Willie!" Isabel put her hand on his arm and saw the first spark of hope she had ever glimpsed enter the disconsolate eyes.

"Are you hungry, Willie?" she asked, remembering her dinner. "I've a great meat pie baking. Will you share it with me?"

He grinned his appreciation, and the expression on his ill-proportioned features failed to repulse her. Isabel knew this was because she had glimpsed the man's soul, which had altered her vision of the outer creature. She felt ashamed of herself.

"Best hurry. The fog's setting in thicker."

They walked out together into a dense vapor that had erased the landscape. Isabel drew back, alarmed. But Willie John bent and picked up the lantern he had left on the porch. The thick yellow light did not really penetrate the stagnant morass, but it pushed it back a bit, so that they could cut a thin wedge through which they might pass.

How moist and bone-chilling the fog was. Isabel found herself clinging to the older man's arm, letting him lead her, grateful for his presence. The incongruity of it all made her smile to herself.

It was not until both meal and lessons were ended, and it came time to cast Willie John out into the blanched night that crept stealthily up to her doorstep, that Isabel wondered with a start just exactly where she was sending him.

"Willie, where will you be spending the night?"

He started to his feet and made a few noncommittal noises back in his throat. She remembered that he had slept some nights in her barn with the animals, but it was cold this night, and so damp.

She hesitated, and he took a few shuffling steps away from her toward the waiting door.

"Tedn't that far into town," he muttered. But Isabel knew he didn't mean it.

"Tonight it is," she replied.

"I can take care of myself, mistress."

Can you, Willie John? she thought, a vision before her eyes of a young, ill-featured child wandering the moors and fens, skulking down street and alley, begging for someone to notice his existence, to reach out to him.

"There is a room above stairs," she said, "no more than a small attic space, Willie, but it is dry and it's warm. I think you should spend the night there."

When he did not object, she knew that he was not only cold and tired, but lonely and frightened. She must make some careful inquiries in town. She was under the impression that he was still doing day work for the blacksmith, but perhaps he had not been made welcome to spend his nights there. Perhaps those men or older boys who had bullied him—nay, half-killed him—on Guy Fawkes night were plaguing him still. Perhaps there was more humiliation and affliction in his life than she could hope to be aware of.

"I have a few extra blankets, but is that old straw tick you use out in the barn there still? Why don't you go fetch it and we'll make up a proper bed for you."

In no time at all, Willie John was safely and warmly established in the rafter room—which, after all, had an outside entrance of its own. *He will be no trouble to me,* Isabel kept assuring herself because, after all, she was still a little frightened and a little hesitant about making herself responsible for this odd outcast of a man. *Yes,* she admitted, *not only frightened and half-unwilling, but guilty. I feel foolish and guilty for wishing to extend kindness and aid to a fellow human creature. And why? Because others deem him unworthy.*

She lamented that this should be so, that she should be as susceptible to the prejudices and pressures of mass opinion as any other person. It made her feel small inside, and weak, and somehow insecure; depending, as she did, upon the frail, fickle, imperfect, impersonal influence of any and all who took it upon themselves to impose their own will and perceptions upon her own.

By Sunday a strong wind had risen to blow the fog away. In Yorkshire the winds were noisy and fretful, as persistent as a wailing child at midnight. Isabel drove into town to attend church services. She knew that Damien would not be there, but she was in want of company and happy to be spending the remainder of the day in Peter Hay's warm, comfortable house.

She was curious about one thing, though. So, despite the weather, when she left the church, she sought the cemetery that stood hard by, looking for family sections and stones which bore the name Rucastle. The wind fretted at her skirts and ankles, but she persisted, pushing grass and wet leaves aside to read the faded names etched on the cold granite stones.

Most of the people of that name, she discovered, had lived here a hundred and more years ago. The name seemed to be petering out, and it seemed chilling to think of Willie John as the last of a long and noble line. Her sight was naturally drawn to the large stone upon which the patriarch's name was written:

Norman John Rucastle
b. 10 March 1808

d. 11 April 1866
age 58 yr., 1 mo., 1 day.

Clustered around it were the tiny markers of half a dozen children who perished within days or months of their birth: *1859, 1860, 1862, 1864 . . . one baby after another, one hope after another perished . . . each paid for with a mother's pain and heartache, her arms yet aching and empty.*

There—there, in the midst of her little ones—a narrow, modest marker with the name *Sarah Ellis Rucastle* carved upon it. "Sarah!" Isabel spoke the word in a whisper that the wind rendered inaudible.

b. 1838, m. 1856, d. 1865

. . . less than ten years later. Ten years of unhappiness? Married at eighteen, her life over at twenty-seven! Isabel bent over the mute spot, where all was concealed and unspoken, and thought of the dim-featured wraith whose sore grief she had felt, as surely as any grief of her own.

"You've discovered the Rucastles, I see." Seymour Phillips stood with his hands clasped behind his back, a comfortable pose for a vicar. His angular face appeared more curious than sympathetic.

"What can you tell me about Sarah Ellis, the second wife?" Isabel asked him.

"Not much. Hers was a short and harsh life, as you might have been able to surmise. Folk about here wondered why she accepted the old man in the first place. He was not known as the kindest of men, and he had forty-eight years to her eighteen."

"Was she a homely girl?"

"Well, she wasn't a beauty. But her looks were pleasant enough and her disposition very gentle and kindly."

"You knew her perhaps better than most?"

Seymour turned up the collar on his coat and hunched his shoulders against the probing persistence of the churning air. "I was her pastor; she needed someone to turn to when the babies came and then died."

"When her husband turned on her, increasing her suffering to agony! Had you no counsel, no words of admonition for him?"

The vicar's eyes narrowed in consternation or disapproval; Isabel could not decide which. "It was all a long time ago, Miss Emerson. Men like Norman Rucastle are not easily counseled or led."

"That is neither here nor there if a man of God dispatches his duty."

"Miss Emerson—why are you so interested? Why are you . . . distressed?"

"I do not know." Isabel felt annoyance, like a painful itching, shudder over her. "Perhaps it is because of Willie John. The man was cruel to him, too."

"Yes, yes, he was. I shall not be the one to deny that." Seymour rocked back on his heels, obviously cold and uncomfortable.

"How did she die? Why did she die, sir?"

"I suppose you have heard the rumors." There was a weariness in the response that let Isabel know this story had been told too many times, chewed to bits by the sharp teeth of opinion and gossip. "Sarah was never in good health. After the birth of her last child, a son, she was slow to recover. She tried to nurse the child and care for him, but this merely drained away what strength she had left to her."

"Did the child sicken, too?"

"Yes."

"And Rucastle blamed her for that?"

"He was desperate to have a son live. You and I cannot understand that."

Repulsion, like a dank mold, crept over her. "You are right, sir, I cannot understand."

Seymour Phillips ignored the obvious and continued. "He meant only to punish her, to exercise the right of will over her, and delayed in securing a doctor."

"That she might suffer all the more for her failures—for the agonies of birth, for the death of her dear child!" Isabel shuddered and took a step back, feeling stunned, as though someone had struck her. "What kind of a fiend was this man?"

"Come, Miss Emerson, do not become exercised over something that cannot now be reconciled or amended."

"Did your heart not ache for her?" The words were out; she had not meant to say them.

The muscles of Seymour Phillip's face twitched; his eyes grew narrow again and this time guarded. "It was a sad business, yes. But all men have their agency, and we cannot control others' lives." He paused. Isabel glared at him, indignant, unreconciled. He let a long sigh escape him. "She was a good and patient Christian woman with no guile in her. And yes, it hurt me to watch her sufferings and be able to do so little for her."

He resented being drawn out this far. But his admission had a calming effect upon Isabel, who pressed the fingers of her gloved hand gently upon his arm. "Thank you, vicar."

His eyes widened; women were certainly beyond his comprehension.

"Will you be dining with us at Peter's this evening?"

"I expect to, yes, of course."

"I shall see you there then."

Her words were a dismissal of sorts. He turned and left her, grateful to escape the raw air and the dismal catechism she had subjected him to. He looked back once, when he reached the vestry door. Miss Emerson knelt on the frozen earth, her form bent over the grave in a yearning, beseeching attitude, like an angel of mercy whose compassion cries out to the spirits of the dead. Spirits, who, his faith taught him, were living still, though in a realm his understanding could not comprehend nor his spirit pierce. *Were the dead aware—in any way mindful of those who yet walked above them?* He wished he knew. Would it be a comfort, or, in harsh reality, a torment, if such were the case?

❧ Chapter Sixteen ❧

NOVEMBER SEEMED A LONG MONTH. Isabel was ill with a cold and found it difficult to concentrate on the lessons she gave and the papers they created for her reading and correcting. Every morning the school day began with the students all assembled for prayer and the singing of "God Save the King." It was a ritual as old as Anglo-Saxon civilization, she supposed. But to her the melody sang to an entirely different set of words, a different sentiment: *My country, 'tis of thee, Sweet land of liberty, Of thee I sing, Land where my fathers died, land of the pilgrims' pride* . . . One day the thought came to her: *Thanksgiving. I shall celebrate Thanksgiving and invite all my friends here as guests.* The notion pleased her, and a celebration would be bound to raise spirits, including her own.

She prepared early by baking mince pies and pumpkin pies and securing a large wild turkey for roasting and stuffing. On the last Sabbath day in November, she gathered her guests in Peter Hay's home, where the dining table was ample enough to seat them, the oven large enough for the bird, and Bertha on hand to help with the cooking and serving.

The meal was a success. And the company, though diverse and modest in number, mingled well. There were only herself; Mr. Hay and Bertha; the vicar and Damien, come down from London; and the elderly Violet Massey from school, who lived alone and was seldom included in company. Isabel had also invited Willie John, which was straining things a bit, but he behaved himself well. Indeed, he was tickled at the idea of being included and entered the house with his hair slicked back and his hands cleaner than Isabel had ever seen them before. In fact, he entered whistling the tune she had heard first that evening at Rucastle House, and again the strains tugged at her memory in a strange, disturbing way.

After the meal Isabel taught her guests simple pilgrim songs and told them stories of John Smith and Pocahontas, and Miles Standish, and described Plymouth for them. They were kind and seemed more than politely interested.

"Some day I shall take you to the original Plymouth," Damien offered, "from which your pilgrims left England."

"I should like that very much!" Isabel responded. "Are there any other places connected with American history which we could visit?"

"Gravesend," Seymour reminded him. "That is where your Indian princess was brought from the ship that was to carry her back to her own world, and where she died."

Isabel had not known this, although she realized that Pocahontas had spent time in Great Britain, being wined and dined and shown off as an oddity. *Gravesend.* The name carried a sadness in its very syllables.

Willie John behaved himself admirably. "You have worked wonders with him, my dear," Mr. Hay congratulated her later, after Willie had ambled off on his own. Miss Massey had excused herself to go back to her cats, and the men sat with pipes, while she and Bertha enjoyed some tea.

"Teaching him to read was nothing compared to teaching him table manners," she confessed. "But he *has* made splendid progress."

"Since when has Willie John become the school teacher's prodigy?" Damien teased. "I thought you could not abide the sight of him."

"I could not in the beginning," she admitted. "But I have come to understand him, to feel for him."

"He takes shameful advantage of your generosity," Seymour muttered.

"Fault me for extending it too generously, but not him for accepting," Isabel countered. "You or I would most probably do likewise if we were homeless and friendless."

The reproof in her voice was unmistakable. The vicar coughed into his coffee and Damien said, a bit too eagerly, "Have you really taught him to read?"

"Indeed!" Mr. Hay answered for her. "I have heard him myself. Can get on quite well now with the most advanced reader for young people, and this in a matter of—how many months? Less than two?"

"He learns quickly. He can also read poetry—and recite it. I believe it was his mother who taught him how to do that."

"Yes, she was a remarkable little thing, for all of her quiet ways, wasn't she, vicar?" Peter Hay turned a languid eye upon Seymour, who answered, almost peevishly, "She suffered unnecessarily, and I believe her magnificent strengths were underestimated."

"I would accept that," Peter conceded. "And I suppose no one knew her better than you did, vicar."

Seymour did not respond to this comment, rather requesting Bertha to warm his tea for him. But Isabel, watching, felt something, and guessed that Peter's idle comment touched on something much deeper, though she had no real reason for thinking so.

All in all it was a good day, though Damien had to leave on the late afternoon train for London, and their time alone together was limited to a brief walk around Brontë Square beneath a sky weeping rain, like a thick mist settling over them.

"I shall be back next weekend," he promised. Then, regarding her with that cockeyed manner of his, "You have imposed an entirely new pattern on my days, Miss Emerson. Are you mindful of that?"

"Imposed?"

He grinned, but then grew uncharacteristically serious. "In all truth, Isa—" he called her nothing but her pet name now, "in all truth, I have never permitted myself to become fond, truly fond of a woman."

"Why ever not, Damien?"

The lines of his angular face contracted as he struggled with himself. "I cannot even tell you that honestly, because I have not allowed myself to think the matter through deeply." He reached out his hand and traced the curve of her cheek and the line of her neck with his fingertips. "Mainly fear, I suppose."

"Fear born of your own losses?"

"That, and more. Take a look around you. How many married people are happy, are truly fond of each other? It seems the few who are fortunate enough to achieve that state are invariably the ones who are cheated by death."

Isabel held very still. His words were like little burning stones that scorched her heart—and the touch of his fingers against her skin was like the warmth of the sun, drawing forth everything that was honied, melodious, and fragrant.

"Isa!" he murmured, stopping himself—abandoning the weakness of argument for the intensity of feeling. "Isa . . ." His lips closed over hers, and she tasted his hunger, sharp as her own, and a tenderness she never had known before—yearning and passion mingled with a love that would not obey his will, but flowed from the depths of his own soul to hers.

When at length he released her and held her at arm's length, his eyes were shining. He had not drawn the shutters on his soul yet, and Isabel gazed—enamored, astonished. *Do not fear what you feel at this moment*, she wanted to say. *Fear will only spoil and alter what it cannot understand.*

But words, all words—all expressions, all importunings—were inadequate. Touch alone transcended. And when he drew her into his arms again, she went willingly.

December—the end of a year, the end of a century, but to Isabel it felt like a beginning. Damien insisted she come up to the city to shop. He met her at Victoria Station and from the moment she stepped from the train, the enchantment of London, the splendor of the Christmas season, engulfed her, carried her out into the streets filled with ordinary mortals, who seemed impervious to the splendor that threatened to unravel and melt the very strands of her heart.

She had never seen such chocolates, such fanciful sugared concoctions, such tops and trains, such stuffed toys, such dolls as the shop windows of London boasted. Here were lights and hurdy-gurdies on every street corner, musicians and mimers, Punch-and-Judy shows, and wistful-eyed Irishmen singing to the strains of soft harps. There were milliners boasting the latest French creations, replete with satin bows and laces, fox and Persian lamb trimmings, and rich velvet fabrics that were like warm silk to the touch. And the bonnets! So many, so diverse, so elegant—displayed in row after row of rolled silk brims with German braid, delicate tucks, silk flowers or ostrich feathers, and elaborate taffeta ribbons to dazzle the eye.

They ate hot roasted chestnuts at the foot of Big Ben and rode in a handsome black cab to the theatre district in the Strand to view a performance of A *Christmas Carol* in the Adelphi, famous for its association with Dickens and his works.

Yorkshire, with its dreariness and repetitive duties, seemed far away. Isabel gave herself over to the brief revels; she was old enough to savor life's unexpected gifts when they came to her. She stayed only one night, in rooms half a block from Damien's boarding house. She saw a glimpse of everyday life as it was for him: noise and bustle, train schedules, work schedules, constant competition, pressing a man to work longer and harder, to be more enterprising, more clever than his fellows.

"This existence would wear me out in a week's time," she confessed to him.

"It's not as bad as it appears; 'tis a certain exhilaration to it that one almost looks forward to. You liked life in Boston, did you not?"

"Yes, but even Boston is much different, much simpler than this."

"So, what do you prefer, madam?" He asked the question in his usual sardonic manner, but his eyes belied his mock manner. "Is it back to the harsh, remote regions for you—do you denounce society, vain and pompous, as forever beneath you?"

Isabel met his gaze with a profound and tender expression in her own eyes. "I cannot answer such a question definitively. I do not entirely know my own mind." She smiled, trying to help him relax. "In truth, Damien, although it is pain to miss Boston, I am grateful to know that I can carry my love and my memories with me wherever I go. I believe I could grow to love any place where I came to live of my own choice—and with someone I loved."

He knew what she was saying. She watched relief flood his eyes.

"You are so beautiful, Isabel. Like some flushed, regal Madonna the old masters painted."

His words both astonished and disturbed her; she lowered her eyes so that he might not perceive the disbelief that troubled them. She also needed time to compose herself.

"What is it, Isa. Have I offended you?"

Some force within urged her to tell him. "No one has ever

called me beautiful before," she said. "Aunt Gwendolyn raised me to believe that I was plain and ordinary, never cut out to be a beauty, to . . ."

Damien clasped her shoulders in a tight grip and turned her to face him. "I do not believe it! What wickedness!" he protested. "How dare this woman mar you by her own bitterness and envy."

Isabel's breath caught in her throat, and she stared at him. Such a thought, such an explanation for her aunt's behavior had never crossed her mind before. *Could it be true? Could Damien—even to a very small degree—be right about her?*

He did not press his point, but his tenderness toward her grew deeper, took on a tone she could not express in words. When he held her in his arms before she boarded her train at Victoria Station, she felt the difference, and it both frightened and thrilled her. He bundled her in with her bags and parcels and kissed his hand to her as the noisy engine pulled away. He stood shrouded in cold steam, a lone figure watching until the last car disappeared around the long curve of tracks.

When Isabel arrived home, she unpacked her bags and tidied her rooms a bit before going through to the kitchen and boiling water for tea. It was then that she noticed the letters Willie John had slid under the back door for her. Curiosity stirred as she bent to retrieve them; she had received so little mail during the months of her sojourn here.

Her heart skipped as she recognized the familiar pinched writing and the return address in the corner. Aunt Gwendolyn had answered her letters at last!

Her letter opener was on her desk, so she used a kitchen knife to slit the envelope, disappointed to realize that there was only one thin, folded sheet for her shaking hands to draw out. She was glad she had sat down to read it, for the few scrawled words made no sense to her, no sense at all. Following a brief unemotional recounting of life in Boston since Isabel's absence, Aunt Gwen had added: "I was shocked to receive your letter, Isabel, shocked to think that you could deceive me this way. Cruel girl, no wonder you refused to reveal your plans to me. Did you know you were breaking my heart?

Did you intend to fly in the face of all wisdom, all admonition? What do you hope to accomplish—what good could possibly come from the irretrievable step you have taken? I shall continue to pray for you, Isabel, as I know your dear mother would wish me to do."

She signed her name to this strange discourse. There was nothing further. Nothing but darkness and confusion and this stunning pain—the full power of which Isabel had forgotten after being these many months removed from it. She sat bowed beneath the harsh blow, her stunned senses clinging to one thing and one thing only: the incredible words Damien had spoken to her on a gray London street, and the way he had gazed—as if his eyes could not get enough of her. She closed her own eyes tightly and concentrated on the love in that gaze.

❧ Chapter Seventeen ❧

Haworth was home. Isabel knew that the moment she stepped down into the station and felt the night air on her cheek. She could taste the cleanliness of that air; she could hear the silence. They belonged to her, and she was at one with them.

As the Christmas season grew closer, Isabel was glad for the ending of the Michaelmas term and the prospect of a month-long holiday before mid-January, when the Lent term began. On the last day of school, she presented to each of her girls small gifts: a volume of Longfellow's poetry, with ribbon-bound bookmarks she had crocheted herself. She was touched to be favored with remembrances from them in turn and enthusiastic promises of visits during the long holiday weeks. Several kissed her cheek as they departed in a flurry of scarves and mittens and rosy cheeks, glowing with girlish goodwill and anticipation. She noted that Lizzie was the last to remain, fidgeting with her gloves and watching the long lane that led to the schoolhouse.

"Have the others gone off and left you?" she asked.

"I am waiting for Mr. Whiting to arrive," she announced, a bit disconsolately. "I let him persuade me to accompany him to York this afternoon that I might help him select a gift for my sister."

Isabel groaned inwardly. "That ought to be great fun," she said brightly.

Lizzie screwed up her fine, slender nose in an expression of distaste. "Perhaps in company with some, but not in company with Mr. Whiting."

"That is a pity," Isabel mused. "How much nicer things would be if you might genuinely like him."

Lizzie nodded a glum agreement.

"Does your sister truly love the man?"

"I cannot tell, mistress! She does not confide in me."

They heard the scraping of boots along the damp hall floors. "That must be him!" Lizzie flew for her books and little parcels, but before she could collect them Morris Whiting entered the room.

"Why are you not ready and waiting by the outer door?" he snapped, not even bothering to look at the girl.

"I lingered there long minutes after the other girls left," Lizzie retorted, "but you are most abominably late."

"Do not sass me, Elizabeth. You will not be able to get away with such rudeness after Claire and I are wed."

Lizzie made a face behind his back and rolled her eyes at Isabel before marching out of the room. Isabel opened her mouth to speak, both by way of greeting and of farewell, but Mr. Whiting had turned on his heel to follow Lizzie.

"Good day, Miss Emerson," he threw back over his shoulder. He had not bothered with the courtesy of turning his cold eyes upon her, either. She shuddered as she watched after him, wishing she could sweep his sour influence from the room the way she swept out the day's accumulation of dust.

Damien was not to arrive until early on Christmas morning. Isabel determined to spend the hallowed eve before in her own cottage with Willie for company. She wished the hours to be reverent and contemplative, not brash with merriment. She knew Willie John would read and sing with her and usher in the day of the Lord's birth with proper respect.

They ate well, stuffing themselves on roasted goose and Christmas pudding, bathed in a halo of candlelight, while the wind at the doorstep soughed softly. "There will be snow," Willie John announced, "before the night's through."

Isabel brought out her hymnal, and they sang every carol they could think of, even some they did not know all the words to and were required to hum halfway through. Willie's voice was not strong, but he did not mumble as much as he used to, and Isabel felt at ease with him, able to sing out herself without fear of censure or even a critical disinterest.

While she thumbed through her books, deciding which poems must be read aloud between them, no matter how late the hour, Willie John picked up the tune—the one that went round and round in her head, like a buzzing insect that she could not catch and pin down.

"What is that song, Willie John? What is the name of it? Do you remember the words?"

He shook his head in reply to her, but the melody came un-bidden to his lips again and he hummed it under his breath while she began Christina Rossetti's verse:

> In the bleak mid-winter
> > Frosty wind made moan,
> Earth stood hard as iron,
> > Water like a stone;
> Snow had fallen, snow on snow,
> > Snow on snow,
> In the bleak mid-winter
> > Long ago.
>
> Our God, Heaven cannot hold Him
> > Nor earth sustain;
> Heaven and earth shall flee away
> > When He comes to reign:
> In the bleak mid-winter
> > A stable-place sufficed
> The Lord God Almighty
> > Jesus Christ.

"I like those words," Willie John said. "My mother used to read pretty words to me the way you do, mistress."

"I know," Isabel sighed. "I wish I remembered more of my mother. I was very small when she died."

Willie John fixed his great eyes upon her, dumb with a pity he had no power to express.

"I should have told you before. I remember certain things; I remember her holding me and singing." She shook her head. "But there isn't very much left beyond that."

The sweet melancholy settled over their spirits, and they sat in silence a few moments. "Did your mother teach you that song you hum, Willie John?"

"I don't remember." He scrambled to his feet; his awkwardness something Isabel scarcely noticed any longer. "I'll to bed, Miss Isabel. I'll shovel a path to the barn in the morning if need be. Why don't you sleep late? I can wake you after I've fed the animals."

"That is kind of you, Willie . . . perhaps I will."

He let himself out, and she heard him climb the outer stairs to his room, tucked in under the rafters, like the lowliest servant or stable boy. The great house on the rise above them stood stark and empty— a mockery of all that life ought to be—with only the wind to wuther through it and nothing but the lament of dead voices to answer the lonely call.

Christmas Day in the morning! All the church bells were ringing; Isabel could hear their faint echoes perfuming the air. Willie John had Pilgrim harnessed to the trap and had trudged back and forth through the wet snow carrying her gifts and bundles, so that all stood in readiness for their trip into town. She was glad to have him executing the path and controlling the frisky pony. She leaned back in her seat and regarded the frosty wonderland they passed through, each tortured trunk and gnarly bush transformed by its white coat. Even the harsh jutting rocks were softened by the sprinkling of snow that sparkled along their surface.

Damien was waiting for her. He helped her down, then kept his arm round her waist as they walked the short distance to Peter's house. "I have missed you," he said, and the words were by way of confession. He pressed his cold lips to her cheek. "You have a regal air about you when you walk," he observed. "I noticed it when you first approached me, floating over the hoary, humped troll bridge like a misplaced lady from an age long gone by."

Isabel laughed and reached for his hand. *Let him think what he likes! I shall not attempt to dissuade him.* "You wax eloquent this morning."

"I stayed up 'til the wee hours writing . . . nonsense! . . . far from a technical nature."

"I am glad to hear it. Your skills at expression should not be entirely squandered in the marketplace."

Why do you have faith in me, Isa?"

"Because I have seen into your heart and know what is there."

Peter came out on the porch to meet them, brushing the snow from Isabel's shoulders and bustling them into the house. His festive air was contagious. A sweet-smelling pine, decorated with holiday finery, stood in the corner, a pile of brightly-wrapped packages peeking out from under its skirts. And one could smell the succulent odors of baking goose and Bertha's hot spiced punch waiting for them.

Willie John came in from the barn, singing the words aloud this time at the top of his voice: "We'll sing and we'll shout with the armies of heaven, Hosanna, hosanna to God and the Lamb." Something within Isabel snapped, like a shutter that had been flung open on a landscape that had never before been viewed.

She clawed at his arm. "Sing more of it, Willie. Please! Sing all you remember."

He looked into her eyes and started over again. "The Spirit of God like a fire is burning! The latter-day glory begins to come forth; The visions and blessings of old times returning . . ." I don't think I have all the words right, miss. It's been a long time."

"Who taught you this song, Willie? Who taught you?" Her voice had risen and her cheeks were flushed.

"What is it, Isabel?" Damien rested his hand on her shoulder. "You look as pale as a ghost."

"I know that song! I remember it!" Her breath was coming hard, and there were tears in her eyes. "My father used to sing it to me when I was a child." She plucked at her throat with long, slender fingers. "He left my mother when I was but four years old, and he never came back. He died somewhere, all alone! I do not know what happened to him!"

The room went silent. Seymour's rough-grained face blanched, but no one noticed. "Do you remember who taught you that song?" Willie John glanced at the vicar and nodded. "Then tell the young lady, please."

"'Twere a stranger, miss, who came to these parts a long time ago. He took a liking to me. Used to let me traipse round wi' him, when he visited folks in their houses. He were a kind one, vicar, weren't he?"

Seymour nodded, tight-lipped. "Go on, Willie."

"What more to tell, sir?"

Seymour sighed. "Did you know this man Willie is speaking of?" Damien asked. "What is it? What is the matter here?"

Seymour crossed the room until he stood close to Isabel. "It may be something; it may be nothing at all. Your name is Isabel Emerson. What was your father's name?"

Isabel leaned against Damien, her hand at her throat still. "When my mother learned of my father's death, her sister, with whom she was living, urged her to resume her maiden name: Emerson. My father's name was Neville Sinclair."

The corners of Seymour's mouth twitched. "You had better sit down, Miss Emerson, you look as though you might faint. Bertha, bring the young lady—yes, thank you."

Anticipating the need, Bertha had appeared at his elbow with a hot steaming cup. Damien sat on the overstuffed settee beside her, and Isabel sipped at the scalding liquid, while Seymour drew up a chair and began to speak, his hands clenching and unclenching nervously at his sides.

"I believe I may be able to tell you something of the father you knew so little, though I am not yet certain they are one and the same man. You know not where your father went when he left Boston? Think hard—anything at all you can tell us."

Isabel shook her head in dismay. "I was too young to question my mother; I was seven years old when she died. My aunt did not allow my father to be spoken of in her house, and my mother was dependent upon her, wasting away with consumption—in no position to defy or even displease her." Her eyes were feverishly bright, but her voice sounded weary. "The only impression I have is that my mother did not share my aunt's opinion of her husband . . . that she thought kindly of him."

"The Neville Sinclair I knew came here as a missionary twenty years ago. His home was in Boston, and he talked fondly and often of the wife and little daughter he had left behind."

"Of course it is him! There is little doubt. How could I have forgotten Aunt Gwen's letter—it was waiting for me when I returned from London, Damien. She wrote the strangest things that made no sense then, but in this context . . ." She sat forward eagerly and repeated as closely as she could remember the invidious lines of the letter. "She knew all along; she knew where my father had gone to . . . and where he had died."

"And why!" Seymour's voice was strident. "Your father was greatly devoted to his religion and was serving a call he believed he had no right to deny. 'God will care for my family,' he said. 'All will happen according to his goodwill.'"

"My father said those words—you remember?"

"He spoke them to me at a time when I was bitter about events in my own life, when I was in need of reassurance."

Damien stared open-mouthed at his brother, but forbore the embarrassment and diversion of questions, and only said, "You knew him well, then?"

"Yes. In my way, I befriended him; in his way he did likewise for me."

"And Willie John? Was my father the kind of man who was inclined to show compassion on such as he?"

"Indeed he was that. But, there was more."

"Dear heaven!" Mr. Hay exclaimed. "We've a mystery of some proportions here! Are you going to be all right, my dear Isabel?"

"I will! If I can contain this terrible excitement that is churning my head into a dizziness. Please, vicar, please go on."

Seymour was tense and pale still, steeled for a most difficult task, like a man walking over hot coals to get from where he was to where he knew he must go. "You remember the stories of the Rucastles, Miss Emerson. The first wife, May, left her husband because of his cruelties to her and disappeared from our knowledge; that is, 'til your father came."

There was a ringing in Isabel's ears. She could not have heard him correctly. "Damien, what does he mean?"

"Try to follow me," Seymour urged, his voice and manner one of patient resignation. "May was a Sinclair before her marriage to Norman Rucastle. When she left Yorkshire, she took ship for America and was known by her former name, as a means of protection. Remember, she took with her a son, a young boy of seven, by the name of Neville."

Isabel put her hand to her mouth. "No, it could not be so!"

"Indeed it was. Your father requested the church authorities to assign him here, that he might discover the fate of his family and perhaps exert an influence of good among his own people."

"My mother must have known and understood this."

"I believe that she did. I had every impression that the two were united in regard to the work he was doing."

Isabel shook her head slowly, as though the new thoughts were having difficulty finding place there. "May Sinclair . . . would have been my grandmother." Her dark eyes grew wide. "Did you know her, vicar?"

"I was a lad of fourteen when she left, but I remember her." He squinted his eyes almost painfully. "She looked very much as you do: great dark eyes, that seemed always to be brooding; rosy-cheeked, but a porcelain-fine complexion. She was a bit smaller of stature than you, a bit lighter of coloring."

"Your boy's memory is admirable!" Mr. Hay barked. "What of me, Isabel? Have I not said all along that you reminded me of someone? I should have figured it out! I am very much of an age with your grandmother, and I remember her well."

Isabel leaned forward, inviting him, and he needed nothing further.

"May came from a family that only skirted the edges of nobility, so Rucastle was a step up for her. She was the eldest of a large gaggle of children, as we put it, and it was her father who promised her— sold her for a price to Rucastle; that was still the way of such matters back then."

"I cannot bear to think of it." Isabel lowered her head, as though a burden pressed there.

"She had a great vigor for life, and in the beginning, she learned to step around him and have her own way. She had given him a fine son, and she was young and beautiful. I believe things could have continued quite decently if she had not gotten entirely on the wrong side of him."

Isabel's head was spinning. "What do you mean?"

Peter Hay hesitated and ran a finger along the curved gray line of his whiskers. "It was a matter of religion. May came in contact—through one of her sisters, I believe—with a rather strange sect known as Mormons. They drew her in hook, line, and sinker. But Rucastle would have none of it and forbade her to have anything to do with them."

Damien glanced at his brother before asking, "Is that what her son was doing back here—preaching Mormonism?" The faces he watched gave their answer. "Then how is it that you befriended him, Seymour? That must have been a ticklish matter."

Peter Hay gave a low chuckle. "There is more to your brother than you might think, young man. Besides, Neville Sinclair possessed his own charm and somehow managed to ply his trade without giving offense—a rare gift, indeed."

"This is too much all at once," Damien protested, his eyes upon Isabel. But Isabel was not listening. A realization had gradually crept over her, a realization almost past comprehension. "Willie John, come here," she whispered huskily, holding her arms out.

From the corner into which he had retreated, Willie regarded her warily, confusion darkening and further dulling his eyes. He would not look at her, would not budge. She cast an imploring gaze in Peter Hay's direction. "This means I am related to Willie—that he is my . . . uncle . . ."

No wonder my spirit was drawn to his. Isabel pushed against the cushions to help herself rise, and moved a few strides away from them, drawn to the window and the snow-muffled streets of Haworth. *No wonder my spirit was drawn to this place!*

"What was it my father said?" she demanded of Seymour, without turning.

He repeated the words again. " 'God will care for my family. All will happen according to his goodwill.' "

"Do you not see? Was it not, then, the hand of God that brought me here—brought me home?" There were tears in her eyes and in her voice, but she continued. "Was it not my father's spirit, and the spirits of my ancestors that called me—stronger than time or distance, or the clouded ignorance of my situation?" She leaned her forehead against the cold window frame, too fraught with feeling, too overwhelmed and numb to go on.

❧ Chapter Eighteen ❧

Isabel did not know where to start first. Part of her wanted to run out and find every person in Haworth who had known, or even met, her father. Another part of her wanted to curl up in a corner and contemplate the incredible discoveries the last few moments had brought.

Seymour Phillips knew where to start, though he still had no relish for it. "Come to the rectory with me," he insisted, "I have something there I believe you should see."

He would tell no more, so they traipsed en masse through the snow-cushioned streets, and Isabel remembered that it was Christmas day when this precious gift was bestowed upon her. "It is not only my father," she told Damien, "but I feel as if I have been given a lost part of myself."

He understood, orphaned as he had been in his own way. Isabel thought the bells rang for her alone, and the sun danced along the fences and hedgerows in sympathy with her delight.

She sat in Seymour's parlor and waited, while he went up to the attic and returned carrying a small leather case, worn and much traveled, which he set at his feet.

"Isabel . . . ," there was hesitation in his voice, "remember the other evening when you and I met in the narrow wynd just beyond West Lane?"

Isabel nodded, a terrible constriction burning along her throat. "Yes, and I remember the story you told me—about your friend who had died there." She caught her breath, and everyone waited. "That friend was my father, wasn't he?"

"Yes. He collapsed and lay there, for I do not know how long, 'til

I found him and brought him here." There was a tenderness in Seymour's voice that was seldom heard. "He was suffering from what he thought was no more than a nasty cold, but the weather was raw that day, and he had insisted on visiting a near-destitute little family to which he had been administering." The vicar's hands were clenched again over the scrolled wood arms of the chair where he sat, stiffly upright and uncomfortable. "There had been much sickness; he, himself, was much more ill than he imagined. Pneumonia set in. He was nearly delirious—but he would not give up the fight. I remember that dawn was just breaking when . . ."

"Did he say anything, vicar? Do you remember anything?"

Seymour shook his head. "No!" The one word was spoken with a vehemence that seemed out of keeping. Seymour passed his hand through his hair. "He did speak your mother's name, I remember that, just before he died."

"You are not just saying so for my comfort?"

"He spoke it three times. The first in distress, the last two with the calm that often comes when a spirit poises on that threshold between this world and the next."

There were tears in her eyes and the terrible aching inside, but Isabel marveled at her own composure. "The satchel was his?"

"I had all his belongings brought here and then notified the church authorities in London. They sent a man down to collect them, but I was not here when he arrived. This was inadvertently left behind, though I do not see how, as it sat in a pile with the rest of the things, packed and waiting."

"Most singular." Peter Hay rubbed at his whiskers.

"I took it as an omen; I felt it to be an omen, though I could not say why. So I fetched the thing up to the attic and left it there for—for whatever, for whatever . . ."

He stood and handed it to her. As Isa's fingers closed over the soft worn leather, a thrill of anticipation went through her. She opened it slowly, having a bit of trouble with the clasp, aware that several sets of eyes were watching her. She drew out a slender notebook in which were written the names of people, some from the Haworth area, some not.

"These were the families he was teaching," Seymour explained reluctantly, and Peter Hay lifted a disparaging eyebrow. Isabel set it aside; thorough examination would come later with the luxury of aloneness and privacy. A slender black wallet followed, containing a few pound notes, a passport, and two very worn photographs. Isabel lifted them out, her eyes so eager that she had trouble getting them to focus.

"This one is my mother," she breathed, holding it up for Damien's inspection.

"Your looks may be different, but you certainly inherited your beauty from her."

Isabel looked again. The small oval face in the photograph gazed back at her. All of the features were finely drawn: the nose and chin almost too sharp, the slightly-parted lips like a child's lips—all somewhat dwarfed by the wealth of dark hair, which Isabel knew had been richly shot with red, and curly, almost to the point of frizziness. And, for all its exactness, the face was a stranger to her.

"This must be your father," Damien noted, "taken perhaps at the same time. They both look very young."

If her mother's image had appeared unfamiliar, this slight, compact man with a dark, high brow and short-cropped hair, rounded features, and a jaunty look in his eye was unknown to her. It grieved her to see nothing but an interesting stranger staring back at her— filled her with a profound sense of loneliness that left her feeling weary and drained.

"Is this what he really looked like?" Isabel asked the question in a small, almost timid voice.

"It is a very good likeness. Try to animate those clear features with the briskness and energy of his personality, the kindliness of his nature."

"Gentlemen, this is quite enough for one sitting." Peter Hay rose to his feet and moved to stand beside her, extending his hand in a most gentlemanly manner. "Come, my dear, I am taking you home."

She did not object. As she rose Peter glanced at Damien. "You are staying on for a few days, are you not? Good. We can afford Isabel this time to herself, then, without too much lost."

Perhaps all were grateful for the reprieve. Damien lifted her hand gently and pressed a kiss against her fingertips. "Come or send for me only when you are ready," he said. "I understand entirely."

She was only dimly aware of Peter tucking her father's case under his arm, of Damien bundling her into the vicar's warm shay, of the crunch of packed snow beneath the wheels, the blown spray from the horse's nostrils: all merged and blurred to her; images that meant nothing more than an ordinary backdrop for the extraordinary sensations and processes that were going on in her mind.

Peter must have spoken to Willie John, appointing him in a very broad sense responsible for her well-being. She knew that somehow the fire was laid, the lamps trimmed and lit, and a modest tea set out for her. She sunk into Edith Hay's comfortable chair, opened her father's attaché case again, and set the two photographs before her. Then she sat for a very long time, waiting for the contemplation of these new verities to become real to her.

In her memory she tried to go back, but a blank emptiness always prevented her, blinking out the vague, delicate images she tried to create. At length she reached into the case again and found half a dozen laundered handkerchiefs in one end with her father's initials stitched on them: had her own mother's hand done that work? One other item, a book. She lifted it out, surprised at the odd, unfamiliar title: The Book of Mormon. She traced the raised imprint with her finger. What had Seymour said of this religion? She could not remember right now. But here was a copy of something her father had held dear, perhaps more dear than his life. As she held it in her hands, a warmth seemed to seep into her. And with the warmth, a weariness.

I will lie down for a few moments, she told herself. The rest will refresh me, perhaps it will clear my mind. She set the book carefully on the table beside the two photographs and went in to her bed.

She did not wake until the predawn, that gentle hush before morning when even the birds have not stirred. She arose, aware that she felt refreshed and eager still. Had Willie John banked the fire and quenched the lamps for her? He must have. It yet seemed a preposterous notion that she and he could be blood kin. She wondered with a sudden sharp interest what folk in the village would say when they knew.

She left the book and photos sitting where she had placed them. After she had eaten and dressed, she went out into the Christmas-hushed world in search of Willie. He was in the barn with the animals, sitting cross-legged at the base of a sawhorse, chewing at a soft winter apple. A book lay open in his lap, and his face was screwed tight in concentration. He looked up almost guiltily when he heard her enter.

"That is a difficult one," she commented, reading the title. "You do well if you conquer half the words on those pages."

With a nervous jerk he rose to his feet, holding the book behind him.

"Thank you for taking care of me last night, Willie John. Would you consider one more favor?"

"Anything, mistress." There was awe in his tone.

"Would you tell me what you remember of my father?"

Befuddled, Willie scratched at his head and muttered something under his breath.

"Sit down, Willie John, and take your time." Isabel spread one of the old rugs hanging over the rafters and sat down herself. Reluctantly he joined her. His eyes looked miserable and uncertain. "You know I be not much good with words, miss."

"Try hard, Willie John, please!"

"He liked people. He were always happy, even when he was cold and hungry."

"What did he talk to you about?" Isabel knew that questions would help him.

"He told me that God loves me, that I must not forget that. He said there were men had the keys to seal families together after death."

"Is that how he put it?"

"Aye. Made me repeat it back to him, every time 'e saw me." Willie John grinned wide, remembering. "He told me I would be with my mother some day. He b'lieved he could promise me that."

Isabel grew quiet. Religion had been key to her father's life, yet she had never felt herself drawn to it. What had Seymour called the Mormons? A sect? What if she discovered that their beliefs were strange and twisted, that they separated her in spirit from her father, whom she wanted so much to respect?

"Did he ever talk about his family?"

"Oh, aye. He had a wee girl at home. Pretty as the moors, he said, when the sunlight played across the spring flowers. He sore missed her, I know."

That was me he spoke of, Isabel thought. *My name was mentioned here, my face pictured lovingly by eyes looking over these same moors where I gaze now.* Her mind could form the thought, but her heart could not comprehend it. *What could have been so powerful that it would make him leave us behind and come to an alien country?* She caught herself. England had once been home to him; this was the land of his birth.

"Saddle Pilgrim for me, Willie, and your pony, too. I want to ride into Haworth." It was time for the odyssey in search of her father to begin.

Damien proved invaluable. With her arm linked through his, she could face the strange, curious faces that would have unraveled her courage entirely if she were alone. He also lent an air of respectability, a validity she needed; folk hereabout did not like raking up old ghosts. Some remembered her father, but only slightly, and were not inclined to stop whatever they were doing and go that far back.

The blacksmith remembered. "He were a bit nosey and pushy, that one, but as honest a man as you'll find."

The apothecary remembered him. "Tried to get me to take one o' them books of his. I told him I had trouble enough living what I did know wi'out asking for more."

Violet Massey was nearly as old as Peter. She recalled Isabel's father distinctly. "He was a gentleman, even though he did rile folk up a bit with that newfangled religion he kept pandering about. He liked to sing, did you know that? Had a rich baritone voice for a fellow small as he was. Most people liked him, I think. Do anything for anybody, and none of the hypocrite about him."

She regarded Isabel with obvious interest. "I can't believe you sprung from the same roots as I did," she kept repeating, chuckling softly under her breath at the thought.

"Do you know why Mr. Phillips befriended him so strongly? If he came preaching an unpopular religion?"

"That was a mystery to all of us. First we admired his Christian example. Then folk became suspicious—what were the vicar's motives? He was our spiritual leader; some began to feel they couldn't trust him." She pursed her lips and lifted her head in an unconscious pose of defiance. "The good vicar's position here was a bit uncertain for a while, I can tell you."

Later, alone, she asked Damien, "Has he ever mentioned anything of this business to you?"

"Not one whit. I hadn't the slightest idea."

"It is all very singular," Isabel agreed.

Later, having tea at Peter's, they told him of their conversation with Miss Massey.

"'Tis true enough, I remember the stir his friendship with your father caused, Isabel. But you know my mettle; I have never paid mind to the rumor mongers or cared a whit for opinion."

Isa smiled warmly. "Thank heaven," she murmured. "How dull life here would be without you."

There were others. They cornered half a dozen or more before the short winter afternoon ended. It was very much a round of the same responses and impressions. Isabel was a bit surprised, even disappointed, that so little emotion was displayed when these townspeople learned that the American schoolteacher was actually one of them.

"Oh, they won't show it to you, not on their lives!" Damien explained when she confided to him. "They'll ruminate upon it for a season, then discuss it at market or over the fence with their neighbor; but they will never speak aught of the matter to you."

She was tired, and he knew it. So when she suggested they shut the lid on the whole business, he allowed his relief to show itself. *There is time in plenty,* Isabel thought. *I have waited these many years. I can savor and anticipate for the next few days, which are all I shall have with Damien.*

They ate dinner at the Olde Silent Inn just outside of Stanbury, which boasted a visit from the Scottish pretender, Bonnie Prince Charlie, and its own benevolent ghost of a previous landlady, when the beautiful old inn was known as The Eagle. Their young waitress explained, with some pride, how the specter was known to stroke the forehead of fitful sleepers, who stayed the night at the inn.

"Have you seen her yourself?" Damien asked, indulging her.

"Nah, but I've heard the sound of the bell she rings to gather the wild cats of the moors, when she feeds them."

"You don't believe her, do you?" Isabel asked, when the girl had left them.

"Not really," he admitted. "There are hundreds and hundreds of such ghost legends scattered over England."

"They don't arise from thin air, though. And if a portion of them are false, that means only that a portion of them are very well true."

He reconsidered. "I had forgotten your experiences."

She reached across the table to cover his hand with hers. "They were real, Damien. And now, does it not make more sense that I should be privy to the Rucastle specters?"

"But for what purpose?" he asked.

"Must there always be a purpose?"

"They usually come to warn or to entreat, or for purposes of revenge."

"Or to comfort and protect, as with Willie and the ghost of his mother."

They lingered over their meal, content in the quiet of one another's company. Isa could feel a subtle change in their relationship since this business of her father had come to light; an acquiescence, an acceptance. Could she be misreading? her own desires creating allusions that were not really there?

Willie John had led her pony home earlier in the day, so Damien drove her out to the cottage. The silent moors seemed to welcome her, regal beneath the silvered glaze of the moonlight. She walked with a sense of reverence across this ancient backbone, this crown of the earth with the wide heavens stretched above it. But when she lifted her face to be kissed, the light seemed to shatter into a dozen sharp shafts and splinters. Damien took her into his arms, but she could feel him draw back. She could feel a protective covering between them, dulling the tenderness of his touch, mocking the longing that trembled between them, like a small frightened bird.

❧ Chapter Nineteen ❧

DAMIEN WENT BACK TO LONDON. HE DID not stay to usher in the new year, for he had commitments in the city where the emergence of a brand new century was a matter of big business and much to-do. All things considered, Isabel was relieved. To her the day was so portentous with deaths and beginnings, change and possibility, that she felt no inclination to celebrate, rather to ponder and pray, seeking the wisdom of the past and the mercy of the Gods to assist her. A new century; a new life. But, what might that mean for her? And would she be altogether pleased with where the future intended to take her? And, nibbling at the edges of her consciousness, like a hungry rat in the pantry was another question: after Damien's strange behavior, dare she hope for a future of which he was a part?

He was gone, but it was not time for the new term yet, and Isabel determined to use her remaining days wisely. There were still some painful, difficult things she had not been able to do. She had made a list of these with "visit my father's grave" as the very first item. He had been buried outside of Haworth, in a little country cemetery along the road to Keighley, where Isabel drove to school every day.

It was not far. So on a day when the thin winter sun appeared securely fixed in the sky, she had Willie John saddle Pilgrim and rode forth alone. She was seldom by herself; she had promised both Peter and Damien that she would avoid that particular danger. Yet she was amazed at the sense of freedom it gave her, as though some restriction to her breathing had been removed. She rode at a walk, drawing in the sights around her, drinking in the clean, bracing air.

The burial ground was but a little scar upon the surface of the great moor. She tethered her pony and entered quietly, loathe to disturb the peace of the place. Seymour had told her that the grave was situated beneath a large ash, and she thought this interesting, considering the affinity she felt for that tree. *Oak, ash, and thorn . . . part of all that is ancient and fixed in this land, forever ongoing.*

It took her only a few moments to locate the small marker with her father's name on it. *Neville Sinclair, b. 1852, d. 1880.* Nothing more; no particulars, no flowery sentiments. He had, after all, been but a stranger, a wayfarer here. *He was twenty-eight years old when he died,* Isabel realized. *Scarcely older than I am right now.* She knelt in the carpet of mulched leaves and laid her hand on the cold stone.

"Father," she cried, "why can't I see you? Why can't I know you? Do you realize I am here?"

She remained for a long while in her cold, cramped position, but no feelings came, no sense of the dead man who rested so close beneath her. She rose, her legs cramped, her skirts streaked, her heart as raw as the rocks at Top Withens when a cold rain has beat and stripped them and left them shivered and bare.

Angry still, Isabel sat down at Edith Hay's desk and wrote out her feelings in a letter to Aunt Gwendolyn, each word a bold stroke hacking at the prison of the past which had possessed her so long.

I came here in ignorance, unaware of the history of either of my parents. But you knew—you knew! It is fate or God, or whatever you wish to call it, which brought me here. But all you could do, Aunt, was hurl unkind invectives at my innocent head. If I had known, if I had come here on purpose, what kind of crime would that be? Have you no compassion in your veins? I want to know about my mother. She did not hate my father as you do. And the people here—they speak nothing but good about him. Who were you to manipulate lives for your own pleasure—to deny me my parents—for what mean, little reason within yourself! I pray heaven may one day pardon you—and my parents, now united, have mercy upon your soul.

Why did I write that? Isabel thought, chewing at the end of the pen. *That is what my father believed, but what put it into my head?*

She posted the letter before she could give way to second thoughts. What a turmoil there was inside her! The long days of anticipated leisure were ruined by this anguish of knowing, not knowing; seeking, not finding; longing, yet fearing; understanding, yet walking in darkness, with no answers at all.

A full week passed following Damien's departure before Isabel picked up the book; her father's strange volume, which she had purposefully left on the table. She had removed her parents' photographs and enclosed them safely in frames, placing them on the dresser in her bedroom where she could see them first thing every morning and the last thing every night.

Now she opened it, more curious than fearful. It was a volume of scriptures, organized much like the Bible, containing books with various names divided into chapter and verse. On the title page, she read, *An account written by the hand of Mormon . . . translated by Joseph Smith, Jun. . . .* She thumbed through the pages idly, realizing after a while that many of the passages were underlined or otherwise marked, sometimes with a written note at the side. Suddenly she realized that she was touching the spirit and soul of her father, breathing from these fragile pages the feel of his fingers and the sound of his voice . . . gleaning from printed words those thoughts and ideas which he had chosen to imprint with love upon his own mind.

She read on, in bits and snatches. The words of Nephi—". . . having been born of goodly parents . . . for I know the Lord giveth no commandments unto the children of men, save he shall prepare a way for them." The words of Mosiah—"Ye will teach them to love one another . . . ye yourselves will succor those that stand in need of succor . . . are we not all beggars? Do we not all depend upon the same Being, even God, for all the substance which we have?" From the words of Alma—"It was appointed unto men that they must die; and after death, they must come to judgment." "Whosoever repenteth, and hardeneth not his heart, he shall have claim on mercy through mine Only Begotten Son." "I wish from the inmost part of my heart, yea, with great anxiety even unto pain, that ye would hearken unto my words."

Isabel sat with the book open on her lap. There were dozens of such passages—hundreds of such passages—and somehow they were speaking to the depths of her soul! *I wish from the inmost part of my heart that ye would hearken unto my words.* She felt it was her father talking to her—felt it so strongly that she knew she must continue reading and in this way learn her father's heart.

Three weeks, and therefore three weekends, had passed with Damien remaining in London, prohibited both by work and weather. January chose to howl through the land with a vengeance. The days were short and dark, and the very air held a wildness. There were many days on end when Isabel did not stir from the gatehouse, not even to fulfill her duties at school. For, though the Lent term had begun, holding classes was often prohibited by the blinding snow that the wind churned into eddies, blanking out landmarks, erasing in its madness both earth and sky.

February came, and Willie John swore the air grew milder and the stranglehold of winter relaxed a little, but Isabel could not see the signs. She did let Willie drive her in the trap into Haworth, not wanting to miss church services for yet another week, nor Bertha's good dinner and conversation in Peter's cozy parlor.

Seymour seemed pleased enough to see her, but later at Peter's, when he asked how she was faring, his tone was decidedly guarded, as though he did not really want a reply, nor anything that might create the least bit of friction. So Isabel waited until the last cup of tea had been poured before asking the vicar if he knew where the nearest Mormon church might be located.

He coughed into his cup and said something vague about York or Birmingham; he wasn't quite sure.

"An attempt to venture in this weather would be madness, my dear," Peter cautioned. "You had best wait 'til spring." He chewed at his shortbread. "A matter of weeks now."

Isabel laughed. "I have no faith in that prediction! Can you be certain spring will not forget us altogether and leave the wind in control, like some perpetual ogre?"

They assured her it would not be so. But the following Tuesday, something happened that occasioned her braving the elements for a cause that could not wait.

Isabel had taken to reading her father's scriptures every evening before going to bed. In the beginning, ten minutes; but the ten minutes stretched into twenty, then into half an hour; she found it hard to put the book down. Tuesday evening when she went to lift the book from its resting place, the screech of the kettle startled her into almost dropping it and, as the pages flayed open, something fell to the ground.

She bent and picked it up gently, wondering why she had not previously noticed the photograph one of the times when she thumbed through the book. She turned off the fire under the kettle and sat down in the brighter glare of the kitchen light to examine the unexpected treasure.

As soon as she looked at it carefully, she knew who it was. With trembling fingers she turned it over. On the back was written: *May Hughes Sinclair, 1848, 18 years of age*. That would be the year she was married! Isabel examined the strong features again, so incredibly like her own: the long slender nose, almost too large for the face; full lips; deep-set eyes; an enigmatic expression—the eyes were not fixed on the camera but looking away, and a determination to the chin, but a softness about the mouth. *May Sinclair . . . May . . . my grandmother . . . my father's picture that he carried with him.* Isabel stood and paced the floor. *Where is my grandmother now? Is she living or dead? Thanks to Aunt Gwendolyn, I have no knowledge of her!* The thought came: *If by some miracle May Sinclair yet lives, has she any knowledge of me?*

A burning spread through her, a burning to know, to see her father's life vindicated. But she had nowhere to start. Nowhere except the old house.

The following morning, riding to school with Peter, she asked about her grandmother's relatives. "Not many of them left around these parts," he replied. "Her mother had been a Hughes, but the Hughes are all settled, I understand, near Gloucester. Her dad was the only one of 'em came up this far. And as for the Sinclairs, well . . ." He thought for a moment, rubbing his frosty whiskers. "There were her dad and two brothers, if I remember rightly. Most of the next generation moved on; you know how that works. I recollect two of May's sisters settled at York. Alicia and—Laura, I believe."

"Oh, Peter! Do you think they are living still? Do you know their last names?"

"I am not certain, my dear. Let me think upon it."

That was the best he would give her for the moment. At the end of the day he presented her with a paper upon which two names were written: *Alicia m. Ralph King—Laura, m. to Bell. David or Donald?*

"You can try writing them, Isabel. Not much invested but a little time and the cost of postage." He smiled kindly across at her. "It has been a long time . . . but then, it won't hurt any."

She tucked the names in her father's book, put away her school things, and went to the barn in search of Willie. Strange how he always seemed to find work to do, even now in the slow months, when no one in town would hire him for odd jobs—at least not until it came time to build, or sow, or shoe the working beasts and extra hands were needed. Today he was mending old harnesses, for which he would receive a few pennies. Tomorrow perhaps the cobbler would give him shoe leather to tan.

"Willie, will you come up to the house with me?"

His brow beetled in consternation. "Gettin' on dark time, mistress." She could not get him to call her Isabel.

"Nonsense. We've the better part of an hour left. Besides, you can bring your lantern." She turned away, saying over her shoulder, "I shall go by myself, if you won't."

She knew that would move him; he did not like her to go there without him. He trudged unwillingly alongside her, his collar buttoned tight at his neck, every now and again mumbling and complaining under his breath.

"I have never seen the upstairs, Willie. I want you to show me my grandmother's rooms."

The hunched shoulders shrugged. "Don't know which those 'id be, mistress."

"Surely you can guess at it. Ladies' rooms—ladies' things."

Might there be something of May Sinclair left for her to discover? Rationally, the chances were slight. But hope, she knew, works on a different wavelength.

The big door protested at the disturbance to its frozen hinges.

How cold the house was inside; cold and gray as the denuded moors they had passed through. "Come with me," Isabel urged, reaching for the banister and starting up the long stairs. He followed reluctantly, but she paid him no mind.

"Which way?" she asked when they reached the top. Willie nodded glumly to the right. The sound their steps made along the scuffed wood floors set flurries of birds into flight; birds homing in the rafters and chimneys—undisturbed for how long now? "Do you ever come up here, Willie John?"

"No, ma'am. I haven't for years."

Ridiculous! Everyone pretending the house no longer existed. Pretending that Willie was a nobody—an embarrassment that would at length go away. And what then?

A floorboard protested beneath their weight and Isabel paused. Here was a room to her left. She turned the handle, but the door did not budge. "Willie," she demanded, "could this door be locked?"

"Could be. Yes."

She tried the next and the next, with the results both the same.

"Come to think on it, vicar did tell me long time since that he had locked the rooms to keep out intruders."

Isabel's frustration was building. "Then why does he not lock the front door?"

Willie John shrugged again and that maddened her. "'Tis my right to come in and out; that's what he told me."

"Couldn't you carry a key?" Willie's eyes were confused. "Never mind. I suppose we must go, at least for the time being, at least until I see Seymour. What about some of the other halls?"

"I wouldn't go down them, mistress."

There was real fear in Willie John's voice. Isabel paused, then marched ahead, aware that he was not following. To her left, a few paces ahead, a second hall ran into the one where she walked. Just as she reached the turn, she felt a coldness, like a blast of air, confront her. She stopped suddenly. Why was it so dark down that passageway—as though night had already descended . . . or dwelt there habitually? She felt herself stagger back a few steps. "Willie," she called out. But her voice sounded weak, less substantial than the night wind that played at the window latch.

"Mistress, come! I told you naw to bide there!"

The darkness, as she watched it, grew denser, converging upon one spot, until the mass took on shape—a tall, looming shape that appeared to tower above her. She could feel the force of its malevolence pushing against her, and she believed she cried out—moving backwards still, afraid to take her eyes from what she knew to be evil reaching out for her.

"Mistress!" She screamed as Willie grabbed her arm, tugging her, dragging her with him. Her fingers found the rough dirty hand and closed round it tight.

"What is it, Willie John?" she gulped. "Do you see it?"

"'Tis him." The words shuddered into the darkness and were lost there.

They were stumbling down the stairs now, half-sliding. She fell onto one knee, but Willie's hand yanked her up again. He had left his lantern by the front door. One hand grabbed it, the other digging in a pocket for matches. When he had the light going he turned white frightened eyes upon Isabel.

"'Twere you called him forth!"

She stood facing him, trembling, her breath as rapid and ragged as if she had been running a race. "Who is *he*, Willie John? You know. Please tell me!"

She looked up the stretch of staircase, but all was still: no sound, no shadow, no remaining sense of the evil that had nipped at their heels.

"I told you!" The sobs in Willie's voice stabbed her with the force of a child's frightened tears. "'Tis himself—the cruel one—my father—who wants me dead."

❧ *Chapter Twenty* ❧

THEY REACHED THE GATEKEEPER'S COTTAGE without incident; both of them shaken and sober. Isabel insisted that Willie John come inside.

"I am sorry," she told him, handing him a cup of steaming tea by way of compensation. "I take it you have seen your father before?"

"Not for a long time." Willie's face was pasty and drawn. "She won't allow it, and that makes him angry. But you have angered him now."

"She? Your mother?" Willie nodded, fingers wrapped around the warm cup. "How have I angered him?"

"You be her daughter."

"Granddaughter."

"The woman who shamed him. He disowned her. He cursed her memory." A shudder passed over Willie's hunched frame. "He used to carry on something terrible. He doesn't want you there in his house."

It is my house now, Isabel thought, and the thought surprised her. "It is our house, Willie John; yours and mine. He is a ghost—he has no power over us."

She could see, in Willie's eyes, that he did not believe her. And she was not entirely certain that she believed her sane boast herself.

Damien came at the week's end with some Mormon literature he had picked up from missionaries preaching from a corner in Hyde Park.

"Strange lot, they are, Isa," he pronounced, setting the pamphlets down on her kitchen table. "Are you certain you wish to . . ."

"Wish to what?" she pressed, when he hesitated.

"Get into all this—this matter of religion?"

"It's all I have left of him! And it seems to have been directed into my possession, in an almost uncanny sense."

"Well . . . I cannot refute that."

"I don't know, Damien. To be truthful, I have never cared much for religion, never felt a strong personal need for it. Now I am confronted with a spiritual system which appears complicated and all-consuming."

"You've begun reading your father's book?"

"Yes, a little." She was inclined to tell him of her experience in Rucastle House with Willie John, but she knew she could not relate it satisfactorily. "Wait," she said, "I have something to show you!" She brought out the photo of her grandmother instead.

"The resemblance is astonishing." He held the picture at arm's length, then close, examining it carefully. "I like her. Something courageous about her—yet look at the gentle lines about her mouth—much like you, Isa."

Unexpectedly, he leaned close and kissed her. "I've been so beastly, these last visits," he said. "Can you forgive me?"

"Of course."

"No, I mean it." His face looked miserable, the lines pinched with strain. "I am not worthy of you, you realize. Rucastle would say it and so would she."

"You are hard on yourself."

"No, I am not. That is part of the trouble." His blue eyes clouded as he struggled to express himself. "You frighten me, and you make me face other issues—issues about myself that frighten me further."

"I understand."

"Perhaps you do. But you are a woman, with different, less complicated demands upon you. Nor have you run away. Look at you here—braving things out, learning and adapting!"

"Is that what you want to do, run away?"

"It's what I've always done—in such a pleasant, hail-thee-fellow-well-met manner that I could camouflage it splendidly, even from my own eyes."

Isabel wanted desperately to make the correct replies, to help rather than further distress or discourage him.

"To understand this is in itself a victory. As you said, men are different from women. Pride is very important to them, and it seems to me they spend much of their energy protecting this tender aspect of their persons, building it round with barriers that, in the end, shut them in."

"You have the right of it," Damien said, very softly. "Barriers that shut out as well as in." He sighed and reached out to touch her. "Isa."

"Could not our meeting be part of this whole providential sweep that has mingled my life with this place?" She leaned against him, her flesh going weak at the touch of him.

"Aye, it could be; I've little doubt that it is."

"So, where does that put you?" she asked, with a flash of insight. "Proscribed into a position you are not adverse to, but do not feel ready for. Some force you do not even understand attempting to dictate your life to you."

"I said you should be the writer!" Damien wrapped his arms round her, hugging her almost joyfully. "Let us leave it be for right now. The day is fair, if a bit fresh. Come off with me, and we shall see what we can discover."

They spent a glorious afternoon and evening together: two young people discovering one another, all restraint and expectation for the moment held safely at bay, the past as well as the future no part of their delightful present, which was sufficient unto itself.

"If you would not mind, Miss Emerson, there are some matters we really ought to discuss, you know." Seymour Phillips stood aside and made a sweeping gesture toward the broad paneled door that led into his office. "Just a few moments while Bertha gets dinner ready."

He had waited until Damien left on the late afternoon train for London, and Isabel thought that a bit odd. She preceded him into the room, more of a well-appointed study than a parson's office, and took the seat he indicated.

"It is an awkward matter we have on our hands here," he began at once, his own large, slender hands folded prayer-like on the desk before him. "If you are indeed Rucastle's granddaughter, then you must understand that this means a very large amount of property, land mostly, is due to come to you."

"What of Willie?" she asked.

"Some sort of satisfactory arrangement can be worked; he is, actually, a closer descendant."

"I would say so, being first generation, myself second."

"Though you are of the first wife . . ."

"Whom Norman Rucastle dispossessed."

Seymour leaned back in his seat with a sigh. "I did promise Sarah to take care of her son, and a promise to the dead . . ."

"Take care of him how?" Isabel, too, leaned forward. "With all due respect, sir, it seems to me . . ."

"You have been here but a short time, Miss Emerson." There was a definite warning in the vicar's tone. "For many years after Sarah's death, Willie John lived with my family at the rectory, and I contrived odd jobs for him to do about the grounds and chapel. Only in recent years has he taken the notion into his head that he would like to be his own master—which, translated, means wandering at will, with no one to answer to."

Seymour spoke the words with distaste. *You cared for his mother,* Isabel thought. *That much is obvious. But I believe the son she adored is very distasteful to you.*

"Did you ever try to educate him?"

"My wife, actually, took that challenge in hand. 'Twas of no use at all."

"Why has he been so responsive to my efforts?" Isabel mused.

Seymour started. "Perhaps it is blood answering blood. Be that as it may, we must address first matters first; that is to say, we need proof, legal proof of your parentage."

"My birth certificate? I can send to Boston for a copy."

"That would be wise. Would they have on record your parents' marriage?"

"I suppose so."

"Then I would suggest you send off a request for these documents at once."

"I haven't thought about . . ."

"About being a woman of property?" Seymour's mouth twitched into an enigmatic expression. "Desolate moorland property; does that appeal to you, Miss Emerson?"

"Are you asking if I might have any intentions of staying on here more permanently than I had before planned? I have given it no thought," Isabel replied candidly. "But I shall do as you ask."

She rose from her chair, then paused. "Have any provisions been made for Rucastle House should something happen to Willie John? Certainly when he dies, very probably without issue . . ."

"The will was both vague and odd. I have not looked at it for years, but I believe the property would pass into the hands then of any living descendants."

"Do such exist?"

"Besides yourself—" Seymour held his hands out, "who is to say? But, not to my knowledge."

"I see." Isabel remained thoughtful. "Well, thank you, Seymour. I am sorry if this whole thing has been difficult, even painful for you."

She could feel his response, like a shudder. "Do not be concerned, Isabel. It is never pleasant to dredge up the past."

"For me it has been most pleasant!" She smiled and took the arm he proffered, reflecting to herself as they began the walk toward Peter's. *It has been most unpleasant for you. But why? There is something more, both to the matter of Willie John and the matter of my father— things which you have told no one.*

"Strangers. Have you noticed strangers about of late, Isabel?" Seymour inquired a bit stuffily. "Uncustomary to have strangers about this time of year."

Isabel agreed absently. Her thoughts were elsewhere. Brontë Square sat hunched, gray, and cheerless, one with the wan sky and the dun, fallow land that was its natural habitat. *What of the leaden and wasted exists within me?* she wondered. *What of the soul, old and stubborn as these moors, carrying their dark taint as a heritage that cannot be escaped?*

✿ *Chapter Twenty-One* ✿

THERE WAS A BUSTLE AT SCHOOL TO complete the assigned work before the short Lent term ended. Isabel enjoyed being busy and feeling useful. She had adopted the habit of watching—looking covertly into faces and wondering what thoughts their careful expressions concealed. So few people had addressed her outright concerning her father, and she did not, in truth, know who had knowledge of her changed circumstances—and status—and who did not. Therefore, she was still fair game for the surprises which occasionally came her way.

"You may look like your grandmother, but I can see him in some of your little ways and mannerisms."

Isabel blinked at her fellow teacher. "Helen, what are you talking about?"

"Your father. Have I not told you that I knew him?"

Isabel sunk into a chair and waved Edna and Dorothy away as she saw them approaching. "If you have questions, girls, they shall have to wait until tomorrow. Helen," she breathed, "I had no idea!"

"So sorry. I thought you knew." With a grin the middle-aged woman settled down beside her. "I was nineteen when your father was here and, as a matter of fact, he made a difference in my life."

"I was being courted by a man I was very much in love with, whom my parents opposed. So, of course I was torn. My family had befriended your father, and I knew they respected his opinion. So I sought him out. I remember the day well." Her eyes, her whole expression softened as she continued. "It was in the autumn, and the spice of ripe apples and burning leaves was in the air. He was raking out the debris in the cemetery for the vicar. He leaned on his rake to listen to me, and his eyes darkened as I outlined my dilemma."

"What was he like? I cannot see him in my head, as you can!" Isabel cried.

Helen reached across to pat her hand gently. "He was of a serious nature, but his eyes were always sparkling, and he liked to sing. Went around humming under his breath or singing outright most of the time."

Isabel's eyes pleaded for her, so Helen continued.

"Let me see. He was slight of stature, but you already know that. His features were dark and well-shaped. He had a quick wit and a quick way about him, his eyes always darting, as though afraid to miss anything that might be of interest. And he liked children. I remember that."

"What advice did he give?"

"'Follow your heart,' he said. Then he told me the story of his mother's life as opposed to his own. 'Much as your parents may love you, they are bound to their time, and you must go forward and make your own way in life. Without love, it is a dreary pathway indeed.'

"His words were so sober. He took my hands up in his and looked into my eyes. 'Be true to one another,' he said. 'Do not take love lightly; it is the greatest of gifts. And be kind and patient with your parents. In part you still belong to them and always will.'"

The air was stilled by her words; the silence reached up to gently enfold them. "He was right, and I have enjoyed a very contented life because I followed the counsel he gave me."

Helen pushed back her chair and rose. "I did not mean to upset you, dear, but I thought you should know."

Isabel reached for her hand and squeezed it in gratitude. "Helen, have you heard any talk? Do the people here resent me coming in and presuming to belong here?"

"Most folk don't care much one way or another," she replied with straightforward logic. "And most feel more kindness than they'll ever take the trouble to show you."

Isabel nodded and blew her nose into her handkerchief. "Thank you, Helen."

"Don't mention it. Have a nice evening, dear."

Indeed, I shall. Isabel watched after the departing figure, the matron with four nearly-grown children and a husband she loved; once a young, uncertain girl of nineteen with her tender dreams threatened, who had gazed into her father's tender eyes and found comfort and encouragement there.

All the remainder of the day she tried to go back—closing her eyes to help her remember. When Willie John came in for his lesson, she asked him to sing her father's song again; she knew it nearly by heart herself. But there were many blank spaces where the words were jumbled or altogether missing, and Willie knew only one verse.

"Did he read to you?" she asked. "Did he ever read from his scriptures?" She held up the book as she spoke.

"I b'lieve he did, miss, but I disremember. It's been such a long time."

"Did he talk about family, about how you two were related?"

"He did that at times. Asked me about my mother and what she was like. There were tears in his eyes when I told him about her. 'She suffered much as mine did.' I remember he said that. 'Two gentle and innocent women. One escaped into life and one into death.'"

"Were those his words?"

"Yes. I repeated them after he left so I wouldn't forget."

"Did he talk about the future? Did he ever say some day?"

Willie's eyes lit. "'Some day I'll come back with my family, and we'll make the old place hum again, you and I.'" The light went out like a candle. "I'm so sorry he died, miss."

"I know." Isabel sat silently, hardly aware when Willie John crept out the back door and up the stairs to his room. *Was it a daydream?* she wondered. *Or did he love it enough to really want to come back and make his life here? If he loved it, does that mean I am free to love it as well? Free to be mad enough to hope?*

When Damien came up that weekend, she made plans to visit him in London during the term break. "I have questions," she confessed.

"I am merely an excuse," he teased her. "You are after this strange, elusive thing called Mormonism."

"You may tag along, if you'd like."

He made a face at her. But, actually, things were better between them. Confessing his weakness had seemed to lighten the burden, especially since Isabel neither chided him nor burdened him with expectations. *Men!* she lamented to herself. *They are far more delicate, weak-willed creatures than women. Especially when it comes to affairs of the heart.* She remembered only too well what had happened with Lawrence once his mother returned to fuel his uncertainties and stir the embers of his vanity. *I must give him room,* she kept reminding herself. *Room in which to grow strong . . . or in which to choose weakness.* She could do little more than this, except to love him. To love him and pray.

March was an ugly month, all wind and black ice, chasing spring back into her lair again, baring its aged, yellow teeth. And things kept happening that seemed to add to the dreariness.

During the last week of school, the headmaster called Isabel into his office. She knew it was for a scolding, since he sat ramrod straight behind his large desk, stubby fingers drumming ominously against the hard, polished surface.

"I understand you have been removing school property without permission."

"Excuse me, sir?" Isabel replied, sincerely confused.

"Lower form text and reading books. I have it on the best authority."

She wondered idly what his ominous phrase meant. "Oh, that. Yes, I have borrowed some of the beginning reading books, but I have signed and kept track of them, as in a lending library. And I asked Mr. Hay's permission before doing anything."

"I run this school." He drew himself up further, if possible. "I am responsible. He pays me to be responsible."

"I am sorry; I see that. It was merely an oversight. Seeing him daily, as I do, riding to school and back together, it was only natural . . ."

"It was thoughtless, Miss Emerson. And I do not expect it to happen again."

"I understand, sir." Isabel rose from her seat before obtaining his permission to do so, and he scowled across at her darkly. "So pleased that you show interest in my work and my progress," she said, turning her back on him with the last words and slipping out of the office before he could stay her, then nearly running head-on into the most odious character of her acquaintance: Mr. Morris Whiting, himself.

His ugly, multicolored scarf slid to the floor, and she stooped to retrieve it for him. "Terribly sorry, Mr. Whiting. Are you here to collect Lizzie?"

"Lizzie?" His homely face was blank for a moment. "Oh yes, Lizzie. Of course."

Strange response, she thought, as she watched him proceed to the headmaster's door and knock imperiously. Perhaps he would find himself roughly used, even scolded, since Mr. Hopkins had been prevented from responding to Isabel's impudence. She felt a slight twinge of remorse for taking advantage of the strength of her position with Peter, pulling rank, in a way, over Bertram Hopkins. But she had been unable to resist. He had never once showed any kindness to her, any interest at all. Just chilly words and chillier looks. Why should he get away with that? Why should he be allowed to sour things for so many? She wished for the hundredth time that Peter would fire him outright. How the spirit of the entire school would improve!

She had not found the nerve to return to Rucastle House since her encounter with what Willie John assured her was the owner—his father and her grandfather. In the light of the day, she considered it ludicrous. But when night's shadows fell, when the black, deserted bulk stood bold and silent against the horizon, prickles of fear would crawl down her skin. *Best leave it alone,* she told herself. *You don't need to go in there. You can wait for a while.* But she resented something as insubstantial as a ghost, a mere probable ghost, having power to keep her from doing something she really wanted to do.

One dark afternoon the black frost turned to black rain, and there were shadows at every window and the cold rattle of wind at the doorways. Willie John lingered beside the fire, his ears pricked like the ears of a trained pointer going after its prey.

All at once he rose, his stout legs unfolding to support him. "It's him. I hear him out there. He's got no right to come here, no right to frighten you."

Isabel shuddered at his words. "What are you talking about, Willie?"

He was buttoning his jacket, pulling his knitted cap down over his ears.

"Don't go out there, Willie. The weather's too dirty, and it's nearly dark."

"He thinks I'm afraid of him. I got to show him I'm not."

"You're talking nonsense," Isabel protested. Then, having to know, "Do you mean your father?"

"I'm not certain, miss."

What kind of answer was that? He pulled the door opened, and she shivered as the cold air poured in. "I'm going with you," she said, but he didn't hear her; he was already halfway across the bare-swept yard and heading toward the high moors.

Isabel struggled after him, calling his name, but the wind tore the sound and dispersed it in fragments. It seemed the long shadows reached after her, or gathered in dark pools beneath her, to obscure and trip up her path. The land was slanted and unstable as it approached Penistone Hill, and Isabel felt herself trip several times on roots or other obstructions. The darkness poured down, like ink spilling from a huge cauldron. She could smell the wet peat, and the seamed rocks leered down at her. She paused for a moment, her lungs burning, her calf muscles aching. She cupped her hands and tried calling again, but Willie John was too far ahead, and he did not pause or look back.

Suddenly all about her seemed hostile, overwhelming. Gulping air into her lungs, Isabel surveyed the desolate landscape into which she had thrown herself. *My people,* she thought, *blood of my blood, have lived here for generations. The wildness has not been bred out of me. I bring to it the sturdy hearts of my mother's people, who laid their all on the altar for a dream, for a chance—for an ideal, which they wrought into a reality they could hand to their children. Freedom. Everything new, everything for the first time. And here all is old, with the whispers of so many tongues from the past that they crowd the air. But I am one of them—and I take them with me, wherever I walk.*

Willie had disappeared over a rise. She would wait for him in the little wind-carved hollow beneath the rock where she leaned. Scooting herself down into the shallow cavity, she heard a sound that at first raised the hairs on her neck—then she smiled to herself. A kitten, a harmless household kitten. It curled round her skirts, mewing plaintively. She lifted it up, then finding a seat for herself, dropped it into her lap. Its fur was yellow with subtle gray stripes running through it. It walked in circles for a moment, the pads of its tiny paws leaving thin damp streaks on her skirt. Then it settled into a very small mound of fur, wrapped safely in place with its full tail, and fell asleep.

Willie John found them thus fifteen minutes later, when he returned wet and red-faced. "How long have you been here?"

Isabel reached for his cold hand and pulled herself to her feet. "I tried to follow after you, but you were too far ahead."

"The little beastie," remarked Willie, as Isabel scooped the kitten up with her, "one 'o the wild moor cats. You want to take it with you?"

"Yes, it is my cat."

Willie John grinned, all his crooked teeth showing, his thick lips curled back the way a dog's mouth curls. "Come along then, the both of you."

They trudged in silence for a few moments, but Isabel could not contain her curiosity. "Did you find—who you were after?"

"There was someone there, miss. I saw his face. But I couldn't catch him, and I don't know for sure who it was."

Her fingers were curled round his hand still, and she didn't let go until she was safely within her warm kitchen. Then she poured a saucer of milk for the cat, and made tea for the two of them.

"'Twere either a stranger, or 'twere him," Willie John announced, picking up the thread of their conversation again. "Either way, I be here to protect you, miss. I won't let no harm come to ye."

"I know that, Willie John." Isabel felt a terrible tenderness for him. "But you be careful, yourself."

"I know these moors better than any man."

"I am certain you do."

"And they be up there wi' me—the sad sisters. When they pass in the mist, they nod to me. Ladies they are, Miss Isabel, like yourself."

Isabel did not attempt to dissuade him. He had not spoken of the Brontë girls for a long time now; she figured they were part of the fancies with which he peopled his solitary existence. But she had given him something more to distract him, to head him in healthier directions.

Before they had finished their cups, rain swept down off the high moors in great sheets, pushed forward in wave after wave by the thin, soughing wind. Isabel emptied a box for the kitten and stuffed a bit of an old soft blanket in it, and the little thing jumped inside.

"She knows she belongs here."

"Moor cats don't usually stay around, miss. They have their own ways."

"This one will."

Willie John took his leave and climbed up to his low, drafty tower. Isabel turned down the lamp until the oil light did little more than cast sputtering tentacles of dusky brilliance across the floor to contrast with the shadows. But Isabel did not mind. She sat in the dim stillness and listened to the wuthering of the wind across the dried tufts of heather, hurling its force against the stout walls of her cottage, making the fire in the chimney place flutter at the touch of its breath. She felt no fear, she felt no sense of disquiet. *I am home,* she thought, *and something within me has come to know that.*

She sat for a very long time, rocking back and forth in Edith Hay's little rocker, listening to the storm and stroking the moor cat that purred in her lap.

❧ *Chapter Twenty-Two* ❧

THE LAST DAY OF THE TERM, PETER brought mail from town for Isabel: the official documents she had been waiting for from the state of Massachusetts and responses to the letters she had sent to her grandmother's sisters.

She tucked them into her pocketbook and waited until the school day was over—until she was curled up by her own fire, the kitten, Brontë, warm in her lap—to slit the envelopes and pull out the anticipated letters.

She perused the lines quickly for content: she should have known her worst fears would be realized. But the resentment behind the written words, so alive still, took her quite by surprise.

> *If you are in truth May's granddaughter or not, it makes no difference to me. Go your own way and leave me in peace. I have lost two sisters to a death and suffering they courted themselves, and I have no desire to resurrect the cruelties of their memories . . .*

This from Alicia King, as the signature and postmark indicated. Not the least hint of friendliness or even curiosity. And the second letter, in Laura Bell's hand, was no better.

> *I know very little of what happened to my sister, May, after she left York-shire, and that is as she wanted it. We all make our choices in life, even if they cause others to suffer and mourn.*

Isabel trembled with anger and frustration, their words making her feel ashamed, somehow, for even attempting to approach them on so odious a subject as her grandmother and the past. *What happened to make their animosity so virile still after all these years?*

There were no answers. She tucked the letters away with her small, but growing, pile of belongings that reflected her parents and their lives, which she had so little known.

It was raining in Yorkshire when she boarded the train; it was raining in London when she arrived. *Oh, to be in England now that April's there*, Browning had written, and the lines made her smile to herself.

Even though her errand was dismal in Damien's sight, he tried to be a good sport about it. He took her to dinner that evening at *The Guinea*, which dated to 1686, in the days of James II. When they were bringing the desserts in, as though he could not wait any longer, Damien asked, "What will you do if Seymour establishes your legal rights to Rucastle House?"

"That does not seem remotely possible."

"What would you do with such a monstrosity?"

"Precisely." Both were attempting to make light of it. Then, with a provocative smile, Isabel added, "It would be the perfect retreat for two artists; artists of the literary variety, of course."

He grinned and laughed softly, and it was as it had been in the early days when she first met him and he was both clever and charming, before reality spoiled the bright image. She smiled back at him, encouraged despite herself.

They walked through Hyde Park the following morning, and it appeared that the rain had worked an unbelievable sorcery. An enchantment of violets and primroses, with jaunty borders of daffodils, nodded briskly in the fresh air. The blackthorn trees were in bloom, and the ash trees in flower—Isabel wondered about her own ash, back home, guarding the doorway. One lawn scattered with bluebells was wearing a faint purple blush as the flowers pushed against their almost transparent green barriers, struggling to bloom.

"Heaven could not smell sweeter," Isabel told Damien.

This is heaven, he thought, watching her, but he merely gave her a bright smile in return.

The Church of Jesus Christ of Latter-day Saints, as the sign announced, had an office in a very fine old building at the corner of Hyde Park. They walked timidly, no, reluctantly, in, and a clean-shaven young man welcomed them; eager, but not pushing, friendly in a very sincere way.

Isabel tried to explain why she had come. The stranger listened intently, nodding now and again, his gaze sympathetic.

"That is quite a story, Miss Emerson," he said. "I am glad you have taken the trouble to come. Sit down here, and I'll bring you a sampling of our literature to look through, and you may select what you'd like."

Damien, tempted to roll his eyes when Isabel glanced at him, led her to the comfortable chair their host had indicated. "Would you like to come back for me in an hour or so?" she offered. "Really, I would not mind."

He hesitated, never dreaming how vital the seemingly inconsequential decision would prove. "Heavens no, I'm good for the duration." He winked at her and felt a bit better himself.

Damien had actually brought copies to her of the *Millennial Star* and Parley P. Pratt's *Voice of Warning*. But there were several additional printed items that the young man pressed on her, another bound publication called the *Times and Seasons,* as well as half a dozen pamphlets with various odd titles: "Joseph Smith's First Vision," "The Gathering of Israel," "The Temple and Its Sacred Ordinances," "A Marvelous Work and a Wonder." And he pressed another larger, leather-bound volume upon her entitled Doctrine and Covenants.

"Go on, take them and read them," he urged, "that is what they're here for."

"Are you what they call a missionary," Isabel asked, "like my father was?"

"Yes, I am." Elder Jackson, as he told them he was called, explained how the system worked.

"Two years or more at your own expense." Damien was stymied.

"Your church is headquartered in Salt Lake City; that is clear on the other side of the American continent."

"Yes, a long way even from Boston."

"Though my father went on his mission from Boston, might he have come from Utah?"

"That is entirely possible. Do you know any of his history before he married your mother?"

Isabel thought of Aunt Gwendolyn's proud, implacable face and shook her head. "It would be difficult to uncover."

"Well, you have his name. You can write to Church headquarters for information, or I'll begin a search myself, if you'd like." The expression in her eyes made him nod. "I'll send a letter off by tomorrow's post," he promised. "You said you had some questions for me to answer."

"Yes, I want to know how your God is different from the God of other Christians. And why you think the dead have to be baptized. And why you are married in places called temples. And why every man in your church holds this priesthood. And what it means to have a testimony." She turned to Damien, whose eyes had grown wide. "Peter told me just the day before yesterday that my father used to say, 'I have a testimony of this work, which the Prophet Joseph Smith initiated. I have a testimony of God as my literal father and the potential I carry within me as one of his sons.'"

The corners of the young man's mouth lifted. "I will be happy to explain for you, Miss Emerson."

And he was certainly true to his word. With simple eloquence, he unfolded ideas that he called principles, things Isabel had never heard the likes of before in her life. To her surprise, everything he said sounded reasonable, much of it beautiful, giving her a warm, peaceful feeling inside. And the more she heard, the more of a taste she had for the hearing; the more she wanted to know.

They talked for hours, and would have gone on for heaven knows how long, except that a man and woman entered to interrupt them. With a pang of disappointment, Isabel rose to her feet and tried to thank Elder Jackson.

"You have been most gracious. We have kept you so long."

"Will you return?"

"I am returning to Yorkshire in two days' time."

"Have I your address, to send on any information I obtain concerning your father?" She wrote it out on a card. "Read what you have."

"I will. I promise."

"That should keep you busy for a good long time."

They walked out, dazed by the late afternoon sunlight, feeling the need, somehow, to readjust to the real world that had ceased to exist for a while. There was much to contemplate, and the peaceful feeling lingered. As they started back through the park, Damien announced that he had left his top hat behind him, so Isabel walked ahead slowly, and when she reached the pond settled onto a bench to await his arrival, lulled by the warmth of the sun on her uplifted face and the warmth of the stranger's words in her heart.

"I want to visit museums and art galleries," she told Damien when he joined her. "All the places of beauty London offers. I feel a craving for them—just as my skin craves this sunlight after the gray winter days."

"You shall have them," he promised, feeling well pleased and soothed, too, by something that was sweet and harmonious in the things which the stranger had taught.

Isabel returned to Yorkshire alone. If only Damien had been with her. He had promised to come at the next week's end, which was only four days away. She had not known she would need him; how could either of them had known?

Peter drove her out to the gatehouse. Here, too, the magic of April had been at work. Apple boughs, heavy with blossom, drooped above them; birds sang from the hedgerows; and the moors, gently undulating into the green, hazy distance, appeared scrubbed and bright-faced.

"How has Willie John fared in my absence?"

"He came to meeting day before yesterday, and we talked him into staying for supper. He clams up, reverts to the old ways— he just isn't the same without you, though I hate to say it."

"That's all right. I know it already."

"You're a blessing to the man no one could have anticipated."

So they chatted the easy distance, and he pulled his buggy up to the doorstep and assisted her out. She found herself wanting Peter to hurry away, so she could find Willie and tell him about her journey and see how Brontë and Pilgrim were faring, enjoying the solitude of the world she had created here for herself.

But Peter was both kind and methodical. He carried her bags to the door and waited while she unlocked it. "Might as well see you settled safe inside," he told her. Isabel pushed the door open, walked into the room, and stood there for a moment or two before the scene in front of her registered, transferring the imprint of her eyelids into her brain.

Peter said later that she screamed and swayed, and he had to reach out to steady her. He was forced to step over broken shards of glass and a mess of spilled oats and flour to reach Willie's body, sprawled near the entrance to the parlor, his glazed eyes gazing ceilingward, hands clenched into rough, bleeding fists at his side.

Isabel never saw it all really properly. Her eyes would not seem to focus, and Peter would not allow her to run to Willie John, or to hunt for the kitten, whose plaintive mew sounded dimly and persistently. Of course, he bustled her back into the buggy and drove her to his house in the village, and Bertha put her to bed, with something strong which the doctor brought over. When she woke up the next day, Bertha informed her a little too brightly that she and her friends had cleaned the cottage—"You can eat off the floors, love"— and Peter informed her soberly that Willie's body was being prepared for a proper burial. The entire experience was denied her, so that her grief and rage turned inward, and she feared she would disintegrate altogether from the terrible pain.

They left her to rest again until Bertha's supper was ready. But she dressed and slipped out, her feet taking her instinctively to the one place she had avoided: the dark, narrow wynd—the alley of death—where a young man, ill and far away from his loved ones, had collapsed and lain alone on the cold stones, and known that he was going to die.

She walked into the shadows, unafraid and uncaring. She sat with her skirts gathered under her, her knees drawn up to her chin, and she wept, making a sound so forlorn that the air shrank before it. She cried for a very long time, until the pain constricting her heart relaxed enough that she could breathe again. Then she blew her nose and sat cold and sniffling, thinking of nothing—remembering nothing and everything at the same time.

When she rose to leave, it seemed that the shadows parted. "Stay with me, Father," she said aloud, "stay with me." And her small, soft-soled shoes made scarcely any sound as she crossed the damp cobble-stones and returned to Peter Hay's house.

❧ Chapter Twenty-Three ❧

Damien came up a day early for the funeral. He did not try to comfort her; he did not, like the others, try to brush the whole thing aside. He did say simply, "I want you to get a dog, a good dog from somewhere, if you are going to stay out there alone."

Seymour read the funeral service, and Isabel knew the tears in his eyes were for Sarah and perhaps for the regret of a promise not quite fulfilled. At the graveside Isabel asked to say a few words, and the vicar consented. She opened Neville Sinclair's Book of Mormon and began to read from the book called Mosiah:

> And if Christ had not risen from the dead, or have broken the bands of death that the grave should have no victory, and that death should have no sting, there could have been no resurrection.
>
> But there is a resurrection, therefore the grave hath no victory, and the sting of death is swallowed up in Christ.
>
> He is the light and the life of the world; yea, a light that is endless, that can never be darkened; yea, and also a life which is endless, that there can be no more death.

She closed the book and looked at the small group of mourners, a piteous knot of souls who had not forgotten the meaning of compassion. "I loved Willie John Rucastle," she said simply, "and I will not allow his memory to perish. His spirit was as guileless as a child's, and this world held no real place for him. But the world he has gone to does. There God, who loves his children despite their flaws—for are we not all flawed?—will receive him, and the tender mother who has watched over him will at last rejoice."

She did not realize that she was clenching the book in her hands, and that her voice was shaking. Damien moved close and put his arm protectively around her. Seymour, avoiding her gaze, dropped the first moist clod of earth. A few moments later, it was all over and the people, faces lowered and eyes averted, began to disperse.

"Did you see her?" Isabel asked.

Damien glanced up at her question, but her eyes were on his brother, and Seymour knew it. "I did not see anything," he replied.

"She was here watching, standing just to the side of that old beech tree."

Seymour went so pale that Damien noticed and moved to him. "That was her favorite place to sit," he said, "when she came to unburden her heart to me." His voice was carefully dull, all expression wrung from it; all but the pain.

"It was you she watched," Isabel continued, "and she looked on you kindly."

"There is no need for you to say this." Resentment flared in the vicar's eyes, and his voice came out thin and constricted.

"I have seen her before, Seymour, at Rucastle House. I have seen her goodness and gentleness. She looked upon you kindly. Make of it what you will."

Isabel turned and walked, not to the vicarage, nor in the direction of Peter's house where they were to break their fast together, but up the narrow lane, under the latticework of trees, toward the open moorlands. Damien let her go, understanding her need and content to wait upon her return.

The mood was one of nostalgia; Seymour could not help but partake of it. Besides, the loneliness of that day had bit sharply into his own heart. And when Isabel asked the question outright, he gave her reply.

"Did Willie John's father truly hate him the way he told me? Did he honestly wish to see his son dead?"

"He did indeed." The vicar sipped at his hot tea thoughtfully. He was here in pleasant, safe company. He may as well tell the tale. "From the beginning he blamed the child's defects entirely upon the mother; no such imperfections had ever cropped up in the Rucastle line before. With the death of his normal children, he grew more and more bitter. When one perfect son miraculously lived, he was jubilant, certain of the gods' favor at last. He changed his will, and since he had made me executor, I became privy to his decision. He altered it so as to leave everything to his son. I questioned both his intent and his wording. 'You have two sons,' I reminded him.

"He ignored me entirely. 'My son shall inherit all my estate,' he boasted and would be drawn out no farther."

"What happened, then? What happened to upset things entirely?"

A grayness came into the vicar's eyes, but he continued. "Sarah never fully recovered after the birth of her son, but Rucastle could not be bothered about that. He ignored her entirely and doted upon the lad, and she struggled along the best she could. The following winter, just short of little Norman's second birthday, he contracted the fever and died.

"His father was inconsolable; he would not accept it, would not believe it! He was in a rage for months, inflicting his pain on all and any who happened to get in his way."

"Willie John and Sarah?"

"Of course, they took the brunt of it." The vicar's voice faltered.

"He used to whip the boy for the slightest infraction." Peter took up the narrative. "Everyone in the village knew that."

Isabel shuddered. She could picture more than she wanted to. "What of Sarah?"

"He confined her to her rooms and then instructed the servants to leave her there—dismissing one after another when they brought her meals and attempted to help her."

"No!" Isabel could not bear it. "How dare he be so blatant!"

"There was no one to stay him," Damien pointed out. "In those days men like Rucastle were lord and master in more than name only."

"He must have known she would die."

"Perhaps he did; I do not believe he cared one way or the other." It was Seymour who spoke again, his voice gray with remembered grief.

"Did you—were you able to see her?"

"Yes, I at last forced admittance. She was weak and raging with fever. I had brought assistance with me. We moved her here and brought in a doctor to see to her." He shook his head.

"I am so sorry," Isabel said. "How difficult that must have been for you." A tenderness welled up inside her, for she knew now what she had only guessed at: *Seymour, the young, very proper, very promising vicar had been in love with Sarah Rucastle. No wonder the promise he had given her festered within him!*

"I suppose neglect could never have been proved." Damien was watching the two of them and wondering.

"Of course not." Peter shook his head and pulled at his whiskers.

"She died, and then Willie John was left defenseless." Isabel pulled them back to the original intent of the conversation.

"Yes, and his circumstances deteriorated, to be sure. I did what I could, but was by and large helpless. A year following Sarah's death, Norman had taken Willie out hunting grouse, a practice he had taken to only that spring. They were crossing Sladen Beck, swollen with spring rains, when his horse spooked and threw him. Even then, it would most probably have been little more than a wetting, an inconvenience, but that his head struck a rock."

Isabel could see the process of his remembering and how painful it was. "But you know more. There was something else that happened—what spooked his horse?"

"The young man was hysterical. I remember his eyes, as frightened as any wild thing. I brought him home with me, but even then it took a great deal to get him to talk to me. Not a word, not a word, mind you, until after his father was safely beneath the ground."

"Tell us, man!" Peter was rubbing vigorously at his chin whiskers with an impatience uncommon to him.

"It seems his father intended to drown him and make it look like an accident. He even told the boy so. 'You gormless idiot! You've no right to be alive. You have ruined my life, and I will not have you near as a constant reminder.' This he said, and many more things. 'I will get me a proper son! There is still time,' he threatened horribly."

"But it didn't turn out quite right." Peter's mind leapt ahead of them. "Such things seldom do."

"That's right. He had apparently driven Willie John's pony into the flood and was pulling the boy from the saddle, when his own horse struck a rock, slid, and frighted." Seymour shuddered visibly. "The gruesome business was over in minutes, with the scared, undesirable son watching his father's life blood flow into the stream."

There was silence. The tale was over; what could anyone say to it? Bertha refilled the cups, and after a few moments, the vicar bethought himself of something and added, "For years, Miss Emerson, Willie John would not venture near horses, much least consider the prospect of riding one."

"I am justly chastened," Isabel replied.

"She couldn't have known that, Seymour, for heaven's sake." Damien scowled at his brother. But Isabel placed her hand gently over his.

"I unjustly accused your brother, Damien," she explained patiently. "It is to this he responds."

"Well. Poor wretch of a lad." Peter sighed. "At least he is at peace now."

"And what of his death?" Damien asked, more concerned than he wanted to show, surmising that the death was in some way connected with Isa, or at least with the gatekeeper's house.

"That is the business of the constable; I believe he is investigating, Damien."

"You think it no great affair."

"I think it a mercy. Yes, I do. If he indeed lives on, how better the next world will be for him than this one was."

"And it is just happenstance that the murder occurred in Isabel's cottage?"

"Murder? That is a powerful word to speak idly. There was a struggle; he was struck—it was the blow to his head that killed him—but purposeful murder? I believe his assailants were drunk. They might very well have seen him entering the cottage and surmised that the young woman was in residence, and Willie John's entry was—for undesirable reasons—"

"Come now, Seymour! Do not be ludicrous!"

"If they were blokes in the first place—out of their heads with drink in the second place—looking for an excuse to rough up someone beneath them whom they loathed, who could not fight back . . ."

Damien turned his head in disgust. "I have viewed the depths to which the human spirit can sink, Damien, many and many a time."

"That is your privilege as a man of the cloth." Damien was really angry. "So, why do you rule out murder, if man is capable of such a catalog of heinous ills?"

Seymour's mouth tightened into a thin, unhappy line. He answered tersely, "It is none of our affair! There are others trained to see to the matter. What can we do for Willie John now?"

"You do not believe that Isabel is in any danger?"

"No. I have not thought so, and I do not think so now."

Peter was stroking his ruffle of whiskers. "She may be, Phillips. A little caution won't hurt."

"But why? It makes no sense. There are no possible motives!"

"Save sheer meanness," Peter mumbled.

"In that case, these villains will give the cottage a wide berth for a good while, what with the authorities crawling over it, keeping watch, asking questions."

Damien rose, his agitation putting a spring to his steps. "Does Daniel Earl still have his wolfhound?"

"She died a year or so back. I believe there is a pup or two of hers around."

"Why does not Isabel come and stay with me again? That would put an end to the matter."

"No. If I leave the cottage now, I shall never be able to return to it. No, I must stay."

"I'll look into the dogs. Meanwhile you must promise me, Isa, before these witnesses, that you will never go alone—not on the moors, not into town."

Isabel exclaimed in protest. "Shall I be a virtual prisoner, then?"

"You will see Peter daily, and you can always drive into town with him. And I shall be here on weekends."

With a sigh Isabel conceded in order to bring peace to the matter. But she was not content, nor altogether certain what her own thoughts and preferences were on her own account.

Damien found his dog, a gangly two-year-old hound: long nosed, brindled-gray, and sharp-eyed as a hawk.

"And affectionate," his champion assured her.

"But he is not my dog. Why should he care what happens to me?"

"He will be yours, after a day or two of feeding him and caring for him."

"He is so big, Damien. Where shall I keep him?"

"He can sleep in the barn. Keep better watch that way."

"He'll just run back to the village."

"No, he shall not, if you give him a chance, show him a little affection."

She knew she was being contrary, but she could not help it. "What of his master before?"

"He lived at the wheelwright's with several other dogs. He was less of a pet than you'll make of him."

"And therefore win him over?" Isabel shook her head. "I have done much acquiescing these past days."

"It is good for you." Damien's eyes twinkled as he began to relax a bit. "Really, he'll be no trouble at all."

"And what of my kitten?"

"Your cat sleeps in the house, does she not?"

"Yes, but he could misstep and crush her—or swallow her in one bite."

"Isa! An Irish wolfhound is known for his mild, gentle manners."

"Yet, he is also a ferocious watchdog?"

Damien roared and came at her, and she acquiesced in truth then, as he wound his arms round her waist, kissing and caressing her, not holding back—not weighing consequences, only pouring true affection from the depths of his soul into her hungry heart.

❧ Chapter Twenty-Four ❧

SHE LAMENTED THE LOSS OF HER FRIEND; she could not help it. Reluctantly, she admitted Damien's wisdom in purchasing the wolfhound; he was gentle as a lamb, and affectionate—with both herself and the kitten, Brontë. The two together were delightful to watch. When he licked her with his great tongue it covered the whole of her face and nearly bowled her over. But with her little pink pearl of a tongue, she would caress his nose and swat at his shaggy gray head with a diminutive paw. Isabel kept Scout, the name the dog answered to, indoors with her until late. Then he would trot out to the barn where his bed was laid. He was company; he was comfort. But he was not human, and he was not Willie John.

Strange, she mused frequently, *how I feel no fear at all here. Indeed, less than before. The changes I have experienced within must be true, must run deeply.* She was grateful for this. Yet, still and all, she could not force her thoughts to venture into the future. Try as she would, she could see nothing but a blank there—a blankness she could not people nor penetrate, nor color with her hopes and her dreams.

She had progressed to well past the middle of the Book of Mormon into the times of King Mosiah and the wicked king of the Lamanites, Noah. There was story here as well as doctrine, but the doctrine ran so parallel with what she already knew of Christianity that she had no desire to fault it. Indeed, there was such beauty of language and expression, such yearning in the words of the kings and prophets, that Isabel herself felt a yearning she could not deny.

It was well into April now. In mid-June the Easter term, and her teaching contract, would terminate. And then there would be painful decisions to face and to make. Her students were already asking if she would be returning to them next year, and their interest in her was warming and encouraging.

"I wish to go to school as long as I can," she heard Lizzie say to her friends. "I am not in a hurry to face what poor Claire is struggling with."

"Is she having second thoughts about her Mr. Whiting?"

"Indeed, she is. But the date is already set, and Mother and Father have turned a deaf ear to her pleadings."

"It is all very well for them," quiet Dorothy mused. "They see it only as getting their daughter safely married. They do not have to live with the man."

"Amen to that!" Lizzie stomped her small, slipper-shod foot. "He can be beastly, I know—all fortune and advantage aside."

Isabel commiserated in her heart as she overheard them. How many women bartered their freedom and dignity away for the dubious advantages of marriage? Security? Someone to care for them? Sarah and her own grandmother, May, flickered through her mind, bearing with them a cold wind that swept clean her girlish chamber where delicate hopes, like violets, clung in the thin, unnourishing soil.

She rode home with Peter. The day was fine and clear, the air rich with the fragrance of blossoms that even the tenacious wind could not dislodge from their boughs. Without even thinking, she whistled to Scout and headed up the grassy fell to where a tight clump of lilacs leaned over the beck. She would pick a bouquet for home and another for her classroom.

The larks trilled close by, and a hawk tumbled above the slick rocky cliffs. At first even the growl deep in the hound's throat did not warn her. Her mind was on other things. But when the stranger approached, she curled her fingers into the stiff, wiry fur and was glad of the dog's curled lip and fierce demeanor. She was as stern as she could be herself, and the stranger took no time in scuttling away from them. But Scout circled and recircled the ground, sniffing and scowling unhappily, and all her fair prospects were ruined. So she turned her steps, with some resentment, back toward the house.

All night the great dog was restless, his hackles up at the least disturbance or unusual sound. She thought to leave him in with her after he had done his duty, but as soon as she opened the door, he headed straight for the barn, barking sharply. She did not wish to follow him, but he did not seem to hear when she tried calling him back. Fear slipped stealthily into the locked and barred house with her.

When she went to blow out the lights, she saw that Brontë's yellow eyes were fixed on something beyond her. She whirled round, nearly crying out. Nothing there. Nothing but the blank pane of window. She yanked the white curtains closed.

It had never really bothered her to think that Willie John lay and died here, where the pattern of her feet walked, back and forth, back and forth, every day. Now, for some reason, she dropped to her knees at the spot and put her hand out, and the small cat pushed her head against it with a long, plaintive whine.

"Grandfather," she said suddenly, "do not try to frighten me. You have already lost. Willie John is safe from you, just as Sarah and my grandmother, and even my father. You shall not bully me. I won't have it!"

She rose, walked into her bedroom, and picked up her scriptures. A cold draft curled round her and the wind started to keen. The cloth at the window was billowing in then being sucked against the cold glass. She hastened across the room. She had not left the window unlatched, nor opened, not even slightly! She was sure of it!

A kind of weak trembling set in as she slammed the wooden frame shut and pushed the latch firmly in place. She perched awkwardly on the edge of the bed, clutching the book to her, aware of a sensation of darkness around her, far too distressed now to read.

Piercing the blindness of her terror, the words came, of their own volition, and without even knowing she began to sing them aloud.

> The Spirit of God like a fire is burning!
> The latter-day glory begins to come forth;
> The visions and blessings of old are returning,
> And angels are coming to visit the earth.

Her voice sounded strong and true, and the powerful melody flowed.

We'll sing and we'll shout with the armies of heaven,
Hosanna, hosanna to God and the Lamb!
Let glory to them in the highest be given,
Henceforth and forever, Amen and amen!

She drew a deep breath. There was no fear, no darkness. She sang the entire verse over again. Then, realizing that she no longer felt sleepy, she turned up the lamp by her bed and opened the book, intending to read for a few minutes. Over two hours later she was still reading intently, immersed in a world that was becoming more and more real, more and more precious to her.

Damien took Friday's late train, and they had the entire weekend together. Isabel realized how good it felt to be able to relax. She had decided against telling him of her night of fright, following the run-in with the stranger. There was little to report, and the man on the moors had seemed to be about his own business and appeared common and decent enough. She would feel foolish indeed to discover he was some inmate of the village, whose family had been here for generations, and she the nervous upstart! Damien would worry any bone she threw him to death, so she let the whole matter lie.

She did press him, however, to speak again to the constable regarding Willie John's death.

"Nothing, lad," the bristly, freckled man told him. "We've no clues, no real suspects. I know, I know—it do appear like foul play. We haven't put the case to bed yet."

That was that. The spring sun made the whole world look hopeful. Isabel held these hours in her hands, like rare, delicate blossoms; fragrant, if brief. But, since the future seemed closed to her, she swept it out of her mind altogether and took her happiness one day at a time.

Isabel had been over to the Olde Silent Inn, just outside Stanbury, taking Pilgrim out for a bit of exercise—Scout perched safely on the seat beside her—her purpose to talk the innkeeper into selling her a pint of his fresh kidney soup. She drove the short distance there and back home again with no incident and managed to unharness the pony and give him his water and oats. He must have seen her at the inn, and in his drunk, disgruntled state, determined to follow her; there was no other explanation except that he had seen her and followed her home.

Scout heard him first and growled deep in his throat. But she was still in the barn when he walked in on her, and she could not bar the door. He carried a whip, a long ugly thing, in his left arm.

"You call that skulking beast off or he'll get the worst of it," he warned her.

She motioned for Scout to come close to her, and he stood like a sentinel at her feet. "What do you want with me, sir?" she asked. "You appear a little worse for wear and ought to be heading home."

"Worse for wear I am, in truth," Morris Whiting snarled, "and yourself at the bottom of it."

"I beg your pardon?"

"Don't try any of your prissy ways, mind you, on me! You hold what is mine, and I mean to have it."

There was such venom in his tone that Isabel took a step back, and the gray dog took a dancing step forward. The tall, lank man cracked his whip along the barn planks and the dust from the straw rose in billows.

"I haven't the slightest idea what you are talking about."

Morris Whiting wet his thin lips. His eyes, reduced to red slits by the effects of too much alcohol, darted back and forth, back and forth, like the hard, glinting glance of a snake. "Claire is tiring of me—time is running out!" His thin voice cracked. "I could 'ave been sitting pretty, if it were not for you."

Isabel decided to remain still; any response of hers seemed to only madden him further.

"You better watch out, miss. You shouldn't have been foolish enough to come back here—'tis a fair warning I give you—and you'll be a wise and safe lass if you heed it—and that's more than I ought to tell you, seeing how sorely you tried me." His voice began to rise a few decibles. "You've made a right mess of things. You got no right being here!" In his rage, he stumbled forward a few steps. Isabel put a restraining hand on Scout's trembling shoulder.

"I think you had best leave now. I cannot contain this animal too much longer."

Morris Whiting looked from one to the other for a few tense moments, then turned and walked very gingerly away from them, as if the pressure of each step he took pounded inside his head. "I mean what I say," he called over his shoulder, and Isabel shrank again inwardly at the coldness contained in that voice.

She waited long moments before walking after him to the entrance of the barn, watching the figure of man and horse become smaller and smaller as he moved into the distance, and it seemed for a moment as if the whole ugly scene had not taken place.

I will not be intimidated, she told herself resolutely. *He is an ill-humored fellow, who cares for no one in particular. And, if what Lizzie indicated last week has any truth to it, he has most probably been jilted by his sweetheart and is in want of someone to wreak his vengeance upon.*

So she reasoned as she rubbed down the horse, straightened the barn, and gave Scout his nightly portion of food. So she reasoned, but it did not altogether answer for the contemptuous threats he had hurled.

At length she went back inside and began to warm up the soup and to cut bread for her supper. Then she remembered that she had not fed the cat yet and reached for the jar of scraps and leftovers at the back of the ice box. Then bending over and sitting on her heels, she spooned the food into the dish, pushing puss gently away until she was finished. While Brontë hungrily devoured her dinner, Isabel absently fluffed the blankets in the little box where she slept. *I must wash these and freshen them up a bit this weekend,* she thought to herself. Idly she pulled at a loose thread and watched it unravel . . . a bright orange thread . . . connected to a green . . . that was woven in with a blue . . . then a thicker strand of a most horrid yellow.

Isabel put her hand to her mouth and pushed the bits of cloth away as though they were contaminated. "Brontë," she cried, "where did these come from?"

The small cat ignored her entirely. Isabel stood and walked the length of the kitchen, her pulse beating at her temples. *Perhaps I am mistaken,* she told herself. But she knew that she wasn't. She had seen that ugly scarf once too often. She had picked it up from the school floor and handed it back to its owner, whose orange tinted hair was as offensive as the florid, ill-matched shades, whose leering face in the barn, only moments before, had made her skin crawl.

The piece from the scarf is here. She struggled to make herself think clearly. *Here where Willie struggled for his life, here where*—Whiting's ugly words came suddenly back at her. *You shouldn't have come back . . . you'd better watch out, miss. . . you've got no right being here . . .*

No right. Those words ran through her head over and over gain. She thought it a strange thing to say. *No right . . . you have messed things up for me. What, what did he mean?*

Brontë sat down and began to clean herself. Isabel watched woodenly. *He was drunk. He did not know what he was saying. Surely, nothing could happen tonight.*

The words, once formed into thought, knelled like a bell of doom: a clanging, insistent warning. She took a few steps toward the bedroom, then paused, undecided to the point of distraction. *It would be madness to try to venture out into the darkness! Surely there was more danger out on the moors than in here!*

But she was unable to calm herself. Nor could she settle her mind to doing anything, to any form of concentration at all. She peered out the window. The moon rocked uneasily behind a tattered witch's trail of cloud cover and a warm cobalt pigment softened the settling dusk. Still she shuddered. *I can't go out there!* The cry was a panicked plea and a little girl whimper.

She paced the floor, back and forth, back and forth, her hands clenched in front of her. *Could I manage to ride Pilgrim bareback?* She glanced at the clock. It was only a quarter past seven. *Perhaps I could make it.* If there were sinister plans in the offing, they would not be attempted until the stillness of midnight—what people called the dead of night.

She tried to laugh at herself, but she could not quite manage. Some instinct, vague but real, pushed her toward taking action. *I have walked the distance to Haworth before,* she chided herself, *and thought nothing of it. It would be ten minutes or less on Pilgrim's back.*

She knew it was not the distance, nor even the darkness that disturbed her, but the possibility of evil—of exposing herself piteously.

If she stayed safely locked and guarded at home, she might avoid it. Yet, something kept pressing her forward.

At last she closed the kitten in her bedroom, left one lamp burning in the kitchen, locked the door behind her, and headed out to the barn. Scout perked his ears at her approach and stood, poised for action, for any word of command from her.

"Will you accompany me into town, kind sir?" she said aloud. "'Tis a fair enough evening for us to enjoy a short ride."

She bridled the pony with ease, but being unsure of the saddle, mounted her bareback as she had so often seen Willie John ride. The spongy spring ground, where even the moist ferns and mosses were flourishing, blunted the sound of their passing. The moon winked a smouldering, burnished eye at them as they took their passage beneath her. All was still, so very quiet, that when a hoot owl's cry fluttered from some distant crevice, Isabel cried out, too, and made Scout set up such a barking that the moors echoed with it.

She had intended to ride straight for Peter's house, but there were lights shining from the vicar's parlor. She stopped and slid to the uneven cobbles, tied Pilgrim to one of the posts, and hastened to the private entrance, with Scout a shadow beside her.

❧ Chapter Twenty-Five ❧

Seymour himself let her in, scowling a little in consternation. "What is the matter?" he said, not wondering if, but assured there was something which had brought her out in the night. When she could not at first answer him, he cupped his hand beneath her elbow and led her to a chair. "Take your time, Isabel, and try to tell me about it."

As she relayed the events of the late afternoon and evening, the muscles of his jaw worked, his eyes grew narrow and constricted, but he broached no interruption, no response, until she had entirely finished her recital.

"You did right to come here." His fingers were twined together in his lap, and he worked them nervously, unable to keep still. He picked up the scrap of fabric she had brought along and examined it closely. "Whiting . . . Morris Whiting . . ." His mind was seeking for something. He shook his head. "What inducement would Morris Whiting have?"

The clock on the mantel struck the hour and startled them both. The wolfhound scooted a few inches closer and rested his massive gray head in Isabel's lap.

"Tell me again what Whiting said to you in the barn."

She repeated the garbled threats word for word, as closely as she could remember. " 'You've got no right being here!' He kept repeating that. And, 'You've made a right mess of things.' Don't you think that most singular, Seymour? I think he meant the gatehouse and Rucastle, not the village and the school, and my being in Yorkshire in a general sense."

A light went on in Seymour's head—a dim light, far back in his consciousness. He leaned forward, struggling to coax the spark into a substantial flicker. "Rucastle House . . . Rucastle House . . ." He stood and began pacing back and forth in frustration, then stopped suddenly and whirled to face her, "Of course! I would never have thought of it! I would never have remembered at all!"

Isabel watched him, striving to be patient as he gathered the tentative thoughts and memories that were coming to him. "Spoiling his plans—of course! *He is after the inheritance and Rucastle House!*"

She blinked back at him, uncomprehending. He sat, pulling his chair close up beside her, leaning forward, using his hands and voice expressively to make her see.

"The terms of the old will, as everyone in Haworth and environs knows, specified that all would be left 'to my son,' as Norman purposefully phrased it, intending himself to be left with one son only when the crucial time came. Morris Whiting is Rucastle's illegitimate son!"

"No!" Isabel shook her head, rejecting the very idea. "Are you certain—can it be proven?"

"Yes, I believe, to both questions. His mother, Elspeth, was a known consort of the old man's. Saucy woman with bold features and flagrant red hair, known as a raving beauty back in that day— and yes, she produced a child, a son it was whispered."

Seymour threw his head back, a kaleidoscope of emotions flickering over his startled features: amazement, anger, chagrin, sympathy, conjecture, and even delight at having put together the pieces of the puzzle.

"He must be in financial trouble, or he would not dare to raise this issue and make a play that, at best, is sketchy and unpromising . . . unless Willie John was out of the way. Poor, useless simpleton that he was; of what use was the estate in his hands? Whiting could step innocently forward—a proven son, as the will states—and where else would the property go?"

Seymour's eyes shone like brittle bits of glass. "That means you were right all along, and we were headstrong fools—back on Guy Fawkes Day."

"Yes. How easy it would have been to dispose of him that way."

"But we—in the form of yourself and your coterie of supporters—blithely and clumsily interfered with him every step of the way."

Isabel's mind was skipping back and forward, trying to sort things into some order. "My absence heralded the perfect time for them to complete what was aborted several months ago, with no one the wiser. Then the American school teacher coming back becomes frightened— hopefully frightened enough to scurry out of their way."

"And if not—if not . . ."

Isabel's own hands were hot and moist with perspiration. "If not, would he and his friends truly carry out the threats he made in the barn?"

Seymour's face looked suddenly ashen and tired. "I believe they would, Isabel; I sincerely believe that they would."

She slumped back in her own chair, suddenly drained, her mind as dull and muffled as thick wool. "The bit of torn scarf—is that evidence enough against him?"

"It should be, all else considered."

"His claim; has he the identification to prove it legally? Would Rucastle's name be listed on his birth certificate as father?"

"Elspeth might have been able to talk him into it; her influence over him at one time was extravagant indeed."

"You know because of Sarah." She spoke the words without even thinking. "When she came to you, cruelly-used and heartbroken, you both knew of the other woman."

"There were more than one, Isabel."

"But Elspeth was the most beautiful and the most powerful, because she had borne him a son."

"That is neither here nor there now." Seymour cleared his throat in his most business-like manner.

"He was born before Sarah died?"

"Yes, he was." Seymour, beginning to resent Isabel, did his best to disguise it and turn the subject again. "The house may be a bit of a liability, but the Rucastle holdings include several mines, and amongst those with mining interest that I know, there has been talk recently of reactivating them. If Morris Whiting has access to capital, he may have some ambitious projects in mind." Seymour shrugged his shoulders, acknowledging all the possibilities they may be entirely unaware of.

"For the time being, however, I think we should take this matter before the constable." He rose to his feet. "I want someone out at your house as soon as possible."

His words, though simply spoken, made Isabel's heart lurch. "I want to come with you," she said.

"To Constable Weightman's? Why not. After that, we shall see."

How used he is to speaking and having his word be the end of the matter. Yes, we shall see, Isabel thought, as she stood and followed Seymour to the side entrance where Pilgrim was tethered and waiting.

They never made it to the constable's red brick office in the village, nor to his house. The first thing they saw as their eyes adjusted to the darkness was a glow against the horizon, like a long spreading stain, with now and again a lurid tongue of red licking heavenward.

"Fire. In precisely the direction of . . ."

"The gatekeeper's cottage!" Isabel clawed at Seymour's arm. "No! Would they dare? All my belongings! All Edith Hay's lovely things."

It was like a woman, Seymour grimaced, *to be concerned with such matters.* "It is you they believe they have trapped inside there, foolish girl." He jumped up on Pilgrim's back with a lightness that surprised her. "Go to Peter's at once. He will know what men to gather. And you remain there with Bertha until I come for you."

Isabel was about to open her mouth in protest, when the recreant moon blinked out from the clouds for a moment, and she saw Seymour's face. *He is worried to death for me!* The realization did much to warm her, but also broke apart her shallow defenses.

"You go with care, vicar," she smiled, "I shall act wisely."

They turned their backs on each other, and in a moment the girl and her long, wolf-like shadow disappeared into the narrow, brick-vaulted wynd that led to Peter Hay's house.

At first she did as she had been told. Peter moved with more decision and dispatch than she thought him capable of. Bertha did the usual, which had been done by women for generations: heated water for tea. Scout prowled back and forth, back and forth, from Isabel's feet to the table, to the window, to the fireplace, to the half-open doorway; then he began the process again.

"Sit," she commanded. But he did not respond to her. His hackles were up, his head down, his ears and nose poised; indeed, every muscle in his body seemed tuned and ready.

"Can you get that gray beast to settle, dear?"

"Are you worried about the men, Bertha?"

"Aye, a little. But my bet is the constable saw the flames before you and the vicar did; he's on his toes, that one. Per'aps he's got the whole thing under control by now."

Neither one really believed that, but the words sounded hopeful, if words had to be spoken at all.

Isabel herself rose every few minutes to pull back the curtain and see what she could see. But the glowing smudge was still there, and she could not tell from this distance if it was weaker or not.

At length Bertha bustled back to her kitchen to do up the last of the dishes. Time slowed to a crawl. Isabel felt trapped and helpless.

"I think I'll take him out for a breath of fresh air," she called to Bertha, "walk up and down the street a bit, work some of that energy out. Come, Scout," she commanded as she walked to the door; but he did not move, did not respond to her. She spoke his name again, then a third time, a little more sharply. But he slunk into the shadows at the far side of the table, making himself as low and little as possible. "This has never happened before. I do not know what has gotten into him . . ."

She spoke the words slowly, half-poised between room and doorway, when an arm came out of nowhere and pinned her arms to her sides. She began to cry out, but a hand closed roughly over her mouth, and she could feel herself being carried from the room, her legs dragging helplessly as the toes of her feet barely skimmed the ground. A moment only passed by, and in that moment, Isabel became aware of the acrid smell of stale perspiration and an almost animal fear.

Then there was nothing but confusion and a terrible pain in her arm as she was hurled into the air, landing on her side, hearing about her the desperate, guttural sounds of a struggle—all in a fog she couldn't crawl through, no matter how hard she tried.

She opened her eyes to the familiar striped wallpaper of Edith Hay's room. Someone was bending over her, someone who looked familiar.

"Isa!"

Only one person called her that name. She moved again to open her eyes, but the muscles would not obey her.

"Rest for as long as you need, darling. I am here. And I will still be here when you awake."

"So you were right once again." Isabel sat in the most comfortable chair Peter Hay's parlor had to offer with her fingers knotted in Scout's nappy fur. She felt sleepy and contented, despite the sharp twinges of pain that shot through her shoulder and arm whenever she moved, and her thoughts were not yet entirely clear.

"I cannot believe Whiting was clever enough to realize that you had slipped through his fingers," Peter mused, dropping two lumps of sugar into his teacup.

"They started the fire in the barn at first," Seymour explained, as though speaking to a somewhat dull-witted child. "When he did not hear the scream of the horses, he knew something was amiss, so he ordered his comrades to break down the door to the house."

"Pity they put that to the torch as well."

"Yes. But someone merely knocked over the lantern set on the kitchen table. For the most part we saved the other rooms and the bulk of Isabel's things."

"Pity Whiting forgot the dog, or discounted him, when he came here after his victim. He knew this was the first place to look for her, that every man in the village would be at the scene of the fire or going there."

"He was angry. Angry men do not think clearly." They all turned their heads at Isabel's cool appraisal.

"Were you terribly frightened, my dear?" Peter's eyes were liquid pools of concern.

"I didn't have time to be frightened. But Scout knew—I can recognize it now—and that was why he was behaving so strangely. Damien, I wish you could have seen him, slinking out of sight of the intruder, but perfectly poised for attack."

"'Tis most probably him's responsible for your bruises and dislocated shoulder," Bertha sniffed. "Me, I was in my kitchen, and I heard nothing until that demon of a dog started snarling like a whole pack o' angry wolves."

"How did you know, Seymour?" Damien was looking at his brother with a respect that made Isabel think, all at once, of the little boy who had once looked up to this man almost like his own father.

"I did not know. The possibility struck me when I had covered more than half of the distance to Rucastle—I nearly didn't turn back." A strange expression came over his face, and they could all see him hesitate. "Actually . . ." he spoke as if the words were painful for him. "As I vacillated back and forth in my mind, an image of your father suddenly flashed in front of me, as vivid as if he were standing there." Seymour worked his large, bony hands together nervously. "I took it for a pretty good sign and turned the horse around to investigate. After all, there were scores of men working their way to the cottage; I wouldn't be missed much there."

Isabel wanted desperately to thank him, but he would not come near her, would not meet her gaze.

"And to think that one of Whiting's compatriots was my own man, Hopkins. At least now the constable has them all safely in charge. I hadn't the vaguest notion those two were related, as well as in cahoots together." Peter was truly chagrined at his lack of intuition. "No wonder the scoundrel did not like you, Isabel, my dear."

"Many things fall into place when you think about them," Isabel agreed.

"Look here, the lass can't keep her eyes open. I think it's time we all left her alone." Bertha stood and began very noisily collecting the tea things.

Isabel lifted her head. "Miss Emerson." She spoke the words as though she was hearing them for the first time. "That has never been my real name, has it?"

"Isabel May Sinclair," Damien spoke the name for her. "Has a lovely ring to it."

Sinclair. My father's name—the name my mother took proudly.

"Isabel Sinclair it shall be from now on." Peter got to his feet, crossed over, and kissed her forehead. Then Damien helped her stand and led her up the stairs to where Edith's cool, darkened room waited for her.

✼ Chapter Twenty-Six ✼

W HAT DO YOU MEAN, HE WON'T SPEAK to you?" Isabel stopped, so that Scout, dogging her step, nearly ran right into her. She leaned against the tall, seat-shaped rock known as "the Brontë chair" and lifted her face to the warm rays of the spring sun. "Damien, you do not mean so literally?"

"I am afraid that I do."

"Tell me about it. What could have turned him against you?"

"One thing only." Damien paused. "I go back to London tomorrow, but I must confess something first."

Isabel gazed into the laughing eyes, a clearer blue than the sky above her. *How do you tell a man he is beautiful to look upon?* "What is it, Damien? Will I be displeased?"

"I don't think so." He sat in the rounded seat of the warm rock and pulled her up beside him. "You remember that day in London, when we visited the Mormon church headquarters?"

"Of course."

"Remember how I left you in the park and ran back after my hat—well, that is not what I went after at all. I wanted some of those materials for myself."

"You were interested?"

"Yes and no, Isa. I was, more than I admitted, but I wanted to see what it was you might be getting yourself into."

"I know the rest of the story," she said gently. "I know how the truth took hold of your heart."

They spoke for a few minutes about the things they had discovered in the restored gospel, those principles which explained God and man's purpose for being here, and how joy was mingled with duty, and growth and hardship with gratitude. Then Damien seemed to remember and drew the conversation back to his brother.

"I told him that I am very nearly converted to Mormonism. He didn't like that at all."

"I can understand. I can understand his attitude—certainly natural for a clergyman—better than I can the intimate friendship he offered my father. What made him do that, Damien?"

"I am sure I don't know."

"It was something."

"Most probably something we shall never get to the bottom of."

May in Yorkshire was dazzling. The crabapple and hawthorn were in bloom and the ground at their feet a carpet of flowers: red campion and wild hyacinth, nettle and crowfoot, and lady's-smock. They had come upon the nest of a chaffinch tucked beneath the gnarled fist of a root and counted four eggs before the mother bird scolded them off. Swallows raced the warm breeze across an expanse of sky that was endless. Moor hens chatted with robins in trees, whose gangly black branches were somehow drooping with a profusion of green. *All this is mine*, Isabel thought, and the thought gave her a pleasure she could not contain.

"Will Seymour get over it—will you be able to mend things?"

"I can only hope so. Isa . . ." Damien's forehead creased into lines of concern. "I cannot say where any of this will lead yet."

"I understand. I feel much the same way."

He relaxed. Six months ago he would not have; six months ago he wouldn't have said what he said.

They walked nearly all the way back to the cottage before he stopped again. "I love you, Isa," he said. "I know that now without question, and I know that our love is the single most important thing in my life."

He drew her into his arms again, and when they were like this, together, the future—though still hidden—seemed like something they could count on, something so beautiful and right that they felt a need to hurry toward it.

"Not too much longer," Damien sighed, breathing heavily, "can I bear to be parted from you this way." Then, into her ear, against the wave of the hair he whispered, "I will not waste too many more of our tomorrows, my Isa. I promise you that."

It was not easy saying good-bye, but all things now were different, perhaps because Isabel was so changed inside. She drove to the station with him, where he kissed her once more and boarded the train. As she turned to walk back to her buggy, out of the corner of her eye she saw someone that looked like Seymour approaching.

"He's already boarded," she called out. "He decided to take the earlier train."

Seymour's face blanched when he saw her. "I am here to meet someone else—a passenger—who is arriving."

Isabel smiled. Perhaps one of his parishioners. She watched a woman, quite an elderly woman, step down and hold out her hand to him. Seymour took the shapely gloved hand in his with some deference. The lady turned her face, smiling, and Isabel saw her own self gazing back at her: eyes large and deep-set, as gentle and liquid as a doe's gazing out from her glen in the forest; a high broad forehead from which was swept back a wealth of black hair—black hair, with scarcely a gray thread in it; full sensuous lips slightly parted; and skin like a dove's wing in summer.

Isabel felt herself running, her arms spread out in entreaty. The stranger turned fully round to face her: the dark eyes grew wide and the lovely mouth trembled. Isabel stopped but a few feet short of her, and they stood and stared at one another.

"Mrs. Rucastle—may I call you that? Allow me to introduce you to your granddaughter, Isabel May Sinclair."

The next few hours could not be recounted, not days later for Damien, not years later for her five children, who asked Isabel often to tell them the story.

Somehow they moved from the station to the rectory; somehow, through the poor, inadequate medium of words, their spirits began to communicate, to question and discover.

"I began to have dreams," May Rucastle explained, "after my second husband died. In each dream I was walking the moors again—myself as I am, an old woman—and yet it was not me at all. There with me, part of me, was what I took to be my own younger self." She glanced quickly at Isabel. "I could not have known it was you."

"Have you not wondered all these years what has happened to me?"

A cloud darkened the older woman's features. "Your Aunt Gwendolyn wrote when your mother died to tell me"—even now she wished to soften the blow for her—"to tell me that mother and infant daughter had both perished of the fever. I believed I had no family left at all."

At her words, grief, like a terrible wave of nausea, swept through Isabel. But her grandmother's eyes, strong and steady, were watching her. So she attempted to smile through her tears. "And with my father?"

"The Church sent word of his death, saying that his personal effects would soon follow. I believed that, too, ended the story until I was impressed to come here—compelled—for reasons that were not revealed to me. My son had written of the kind and generous young vicar, so when I was prompted to come back, I made inquiries through him."

"Why did you not tell me, Seymour?"

Seymour ignored the accusation in Isabel's tone and defended himself briefly. "Her letter barely proceeded her, Miss Sinclair. It arrived but three days ago, and I thought it best to wait and let you see for yourself, rather than shock you further at this particular time with news of her."

"I had no idea where you were, if you were living or dead."

"I made it from here to Liverpool, from Liverpool to New York, from New York to the valleys of the mountains; myself alone with my little son."

"Then you did live in Salt Lake City?"

"The Logan valley, not far from there."

"Then, how did Father meet my mother?"

"He went back east to study; he had earned a scholarship at Boston College."

Isabel started, her color high. "I also studied there," she informed her grandmother proudly.

"There is so much, so very much," May Rucastle murmured, "for both of us to learn."

"My mother . . ."

"I never met your mother. Her health was poor when they married. She did not possess the endurance, nor he the money, for them to make the difficult trip. But I know she loved your father, and she loved his religion when she embraced it."

Curiosity, like a parching thirst, rose up in Isabel. "After my father left her, she was little more than a prisoner, having to answer to all of my aunt's whims and demands. It must have been horrible for her. My aunt forbade her to mention my father's name or the word *Mormonism*, or she would put her out of the house."

Isabel's voice trembled as she spoke, but for the first time in her life she took no heed of it, allowing her heart to express itself, with no fears, no holding back.

"We know too little of one another and the past that is part of us. But I am content that we shall uncover more. Why else was I prompted to return? Why else did the Spirit see fit to unite us, if he had not joy in store?"

There was too much, too much to grasp and take in all at once. But May turned to the vicar and asked one sober question: "Tell me how my son died."

Seymour's entire visage tightened into lines of distress, and his face paled. But he told detail by detail of the last few days of Neville Sinclair's life. When the vicar reached the point of her father's death, Isabel reached over and clasped her grandmother's hand. But her eyes were watching Seymour carefully, sensing something, as she had the first time.

"He said something to you. I know it. Tell me this time, Seymour."

"You have no right to pry into such matters. What passed then was my affair."

"And it was bound up with Sarah and your love for her, and you have carried the burden alone for these many years."

Isabel watched the struggle play over his features. She sat very still, waiting, praying.

"You have, with that irksome insight of yours, Isabel, discovered the primary reason for our friendship. I had turned to your father for counsel and comfort. Being a man of the cloth, whom else could I with any degree of safety consult? I had come to love Sarah deeply, despite the apparent 'wrongness' of doing so. Nothing untoward happened between us; it wasn't like that. I was a lad of twenty when Rucastle married her in '56."

"The year after I left him." Mary's voice was soft with irony. "He did not waste much time."

"Aye, but she was even younger than yourself, ma'am, and him getting every year older—and meaner."

"You were approaching thirty at the time of your association with her, at the time of her death." Isabel wanted to get back to the basic gist of the conversation.

"Yes, and married by then, with one small daughter." The defensiveness in his tone was unmistakable. Isabel's heart went out to him.

"Your feelings for Sarah were understandable," she said, unable to help herself, "founded initially on an admirable and understandable sympathy."

"I was in love with her."

He will not go easy on himself. Isabel sighed.

"What did my son say to you?"

"You must understand that it was his hope to convert me to Mormonism." The words were distasteful in Seymour's mouth. "I was distraught at his dying, and he was attempting to make light a bit.

" 'I will come back to you some day, in one form or another, to haunt you,' he said and smiled. I remember the beauty of that smile. He continued more seriously. 'I will bring you peace, if you will have it.' Those were the last real words he said, before death claimed his attention altogether, save for your mother's name at the very end."

Isabel felt her grandmother's fingers tighten over her own, and knew she was crying inside, weeping where her tears were not visible.

"It is all right, Seymour," Isabel said. "Why are you afraid still? Why do you fight it? He has come back as he promised, you know."

"Yes, I have understood that from the beginning, from the first day I learned who you were."

"Things will be all right, Seymour." She had not meant to repeat the words and, as it was, she spoke them under her breath. "Things of this nature do not happen for naught. Your Heavenly Father is mindful of you."

"That is why he brings division in my house, while he unites your own?"

May did not understand what things they spoke of, but her eyes were bright, both with interest and sympathy. "Peace comes from knowing oneself, from being reconciled to both the best and the worst within you."

"Mormons are the only people," Seymour grimaced a little, "who take it upon themselves to preach to a minister."

May rose. "I am anxious to see the old house. Who is in possession of it now?"

"That, in itself, is a long, somewhat tragic story." Isabel sighed.

"Your granddaughter, for all intents and purposes, is in possession of the property now."

May's eyebrows shot upward. *What a handsome woman she still is,* Isabel marveled. *Her trials and losses, though severe, have not conquered her. Unlike myself, unlike Damien, or even Seymour, she knows who she is. My father must have been like that . . . and my mother, coming of noble New England stock . . . if she was too timid to mingle the old and the new, at least she took the first steps—for herself and for me. I can go on from here, in a way both of them would want me to.*

Seymour walked to the door with them. Isabel leaned over and kissed his cheek gently, and he did not protest nor draw back.

"Yorkshire is beautiful, isn't it?" May Sinclair Rucastle drew in a deep breath of the clean, peat-rich air. "I did not think to see it again in this life."

"I did not think to ever set eyes on you." Isabel felt a sense of well-being rise up within her. *I have never even known what happiness is,* she marveled. *But I have been learning to recognize it, to cultivate it these past months since I have been here.* She remembered the peace she had felt about the future, as though it would somehow take care of itself. *Faith . . . was this the beginnings of faith?* she wondered. *I have so much to learn!*

"My trap is waiting," Isabel said.

"Good," her grandmother answered, "the day is fine, and I do not feel in the least bit tired. Let us go to Rucastle House together, granddaughter." She placed her gloved hand lightly on Isabel's arm and dark eyes gazed into dark eyes; spirit communicating with spirit. "Come, Isabel, I will take you home."